The May Spoon

The
MAY SPOON

a novel by
A. CARLEON

BEAUFORT BOOKS, INC.
New York · Toronto

Library of Congress Cataloging in Publication Data

Carleon, A., 1922–
The May spoon.
Summary: A young girl has major difficulties
keeping up with her not-so-ordinary family.
[1. Family life—Fiction]   I. Title.
PZ7.C21478May   [Fic]   81-6101
ISBN 0-8253-0059-2   AACR2

Published in the United States by Beaufort Books, Inc.,
New York. Published simultaneously in Canada by
General Publishing Co. Limited

Designer: Ellen LoGiudice
Printed in the U.S.A.   First Edition
10   9   8   7   6   5   4   3   2   1

To my beloved sisty ugler,
Eileen O'Grady Logie
From her affectionate Indercella

*I*f there's a worse name in the whole world than mine, I'd like to hear it. If you stop to think of it, you'd have to sort of hate somebody to call them Isabel McMurry.

No matter what you do with it, it doesn't come out any better. I've tried. I tried Ysobel, Isobelle, Isabella, and once even Jezebel. He (my father) laughed so hard at that one I knew there must be something wrong with it.

Names are very important. I read that people in South America don't call their kids Pasquale anymore because that's what Donald Duck is called in Spanish.

Some people can change their names just a bit and get away with it. Look at Beatrice Featherstone. Now, the name Beatrice is really just as rotten as Isabel, but hers is pronounced Bee-ya-tree-chee, just like it is in Italian, and everybody, when they hear it, says what a beautiful name. Her mother and father spent their honeymoon in Florence or Venice or someplace and they named her after Dante and Beatrice.

Well, I am not going to get stuck with Isabel. I am going to use my grandmother's maiden name, Ann Carleon, which is very beautiful and sure beats Beatrice Featherstone.

This is my diary. I've been thinking about it a lot and I believe most of the people who keep them are hoping someone will find their diary in an old attic someday and they'll be immortal. That's sort of what I have in mind.

I mean, who wants to write and have nobody ever read it? It's not natural. But the trouble with diaries is that they ought to be like stories. A good story rolls along like a good recipe, with a little bit of pepper here and a bit of sugar or spice there, but *nothing* ever happens to me. Life is all flour with no seasoning. Just one big blah.

Who cares if I got up this morning, brushed my teeth and went to school or didn't? I know I don't. On the other hand, if I lie, (which I have an awful tendency to do) and put in interesting things that didn't happen, then it isn't a diary. I suppose I could stick to the truth and produce the dreariest volume ever written, or I can sort of stretch the truth and touch it up with a few colorful nice little lies, just enough to keep us both interested.

Well, I've thought it over for a long time, and dull as my life may be, because nothing has ever happened to me, and probably nothing ever will happen to me, I will tell the truth. I have a tendency to forget what I've said, and if I write down the truth, then when I am aged, I'll know everything exactly as it was, even if it's not how other people saw it happen.

I live in West Vancouver with my father and mother, Mr. and Mrs. McMurry, and my older sister, Marian, who I usually call Fatso.

The time we spend together is mostly at the table, and it's always the same old thing.

My father sits at the head of the table and rants on about me not eating and all the starving children in Bangladesh, while old Fatso sits across from me filling her face until He starts in on her for what He calls the Glutton Syndrome. She, my mother, sits at the other end of the table and smiles at all of us, especially at Bud's empty place, which isn't really empty because we set a place for him every night.

Bud is dead.

After dinner it's also the same old thing. She says, "Buddy is late tonight. Isabel dear, you might as well give his dinner to Peggy."

So, I take the full plate onto the back porch and scrape it into Peggy's dish. After dinner old Fatso and I have a fight over who is going to wash the dishes and who is going to dry. We are supposed to do it by turns but she cheats.

Then He comes in and yells that's enough of that, can't He have any peace and quiet in His own house. Fatso always plays up to Him and says, "I'm sorry, Daddy, but Isabel never takes her turn properly," and I say I do so and there we are again. Although last week He got mad at her and when she said Daddy, why can't we get a dishwasher like everybody else, He tossed the dishcloth at her and said that's the only dishwasher we need in this house. All it requires is an elbow to move it.

It serves her right. Ever since she got her driver's license three months ago she acts even worse than usual, as if she's a real grown-up, even though she's only allowed to drive Mumma shopping or me to the dentist or Peggy to the vet's.

As you have probably guessed by now, mealtimes are not fun occasions in our house. I always remember how to spell occasion because my English teacher, Miss Swanson said, "There is never any occasion to make an ass out of yourself." Get it?

What with Him and His table manners, (last week She

forgot to put clean napkins on the table so He wiped his mouth on the tablecloth out of sheer meanness) and Her sitting beaming at where Bud isn't and Fatso eating as if she's about to be shipped off to Bangladesh, it's enough to take anyone's appetite away.

I am one hundred pounds underweight.

He told Fatso gluttony was one of the seven deadly sins and she said she bet it was one of the most acceptable because it didn't hurt anybody else and He said yes, she was a bright girl and He hadn't thought of it that way. It's sickening the way she plays up to him. You just try eating here.

On top of everything else, most of the time She is a very good cook but She tends to forget a lot. Last week it was rhubarb pie with no sugar in it. Well, you can imagine what that tasted like but He gave me that eat-it-or-I'll-kill-you look, so I did. Fatso romped through two pieces and didn't even notice.

Yesterday I went to the Mall in Park Royal. The Mall is supposed to be the most beautiful in Canada. If you like malls, I guess. Anyhow, there was nothing else to do. The Mall is covered with stores going in all directions, fountains, pools, piped-in music, fake trees, flowers and benches and restaurants. It's about as natural as Disneyland, which, of course, I have only seen on TV, because we never go anywhere, but I often mosey down there when I'm tired of me. I never have much money to spend, but I can always use up a rotten afternoon walking and looking at the people and in the store windows.

There are all sorts of specialty shops, which make it quite interesting. For five minutes before you get to it, you can smell a shop that imports different coffees. And there are stores that sell nothing but clocks, or antiques, or just wax and dried flowers, or candy or scarves, or records or books or toys. There's even a shop that sells only wooden kitchen tools and appliances. And it's all free to look at.

Well, there I was, walking along, when I met a lady who was handing out religious pamphlets. I started talking to her and we had a very enlightening conversation. I told her I wanted to pray to make my mother better, but I really didn't know quite how to go about it, as I had never had any religious instruction.

This lady's name was Mrs. Lamb and she said Jesus was my friend, and, like any friend, I could talk to him and ask him for anything anytime I wanted, even right in the the Mall.

I asked if she was sure He would hear me and she said He doesn't always answer our prayers just when we want them, or, for that matter, the way we want them, which struck me as not being of much use.

Anyway, she gave me some literature to read and from what I can make of it, the world is about to end because we are wicked, but some will be saved because they heeded the Word. It doesn't say just *when* the world is going to end. If it's a hundred years from now I think I'd rather just go on being a sinner. But of course, for my mother's sake, I've got to get down to business.

If only my father went out to work like other fathers, away from the house. But no. The entire third story of our house is made over into a suite for Him to work in. It is kept locked, like Bluebeard's castle, and only He has the key.

But yesterday we had a break in our usual dull routine. One of his loony friends from England visited us. He told us and then looked right at me and said,

"I will be serving him a drink in the living room before taking him upstairs. You and Marian will be introduced to him in the living room. And you, Isabel, will say how do you do and nothing else. Do I make myself absolutely clear? We will not have a repeat of your last performance when I entertained. Am I understood?"

I nodded.

He said, "Say 'yes,' loudly and distinctly."

So I said yes, loudly and distinctly.

This tubby little guy with a pointed white beard and wearing tweeds that smelled like Peggy turned up.

We were all in the living room, then He went to the kitchen to mix the drinks. Mumma sat quietly in a corner with her hands folded on her lap and her usual sweet smile on her face, waiting patiently for Bud, and Marian was standing next to the fireplace with Professor Halden.

He said, "How fortunate Chawz is to be surrounded by this charming seraglio."

I didn't know what a seraglio was, although I looked it up later in the dictionary. I smiled politely but Marian had a most peculiar look on her face.

She and the Professor were standing with their backs to the fireside and they were facing the room and she swears (although she said don't, for God's sake, tell Him) that all the time Professor Halden was beaming innocently at us, he was pinching her bum. She says he is a very dirty old man. Now I can't prove that he did this, of course, but unlike me, Marian very seldom tells lies.

After their drinks He and the Professor went upstairs and I went off to look up seraglio in the dictionary.

It's a harem, the women's apartments in a Muhammadan household.

When they came down the Professor, who is a political economist and should know better than to go around pinching girls' bottoms, said, "How inspirational, Chawz, how absolutely inspirational to write in such surroundings. The quiet, the view of the ocean. It is all quite stunning."

Marian said later stunned would be a better word if He knew what that dirty little man had been up to.

He said yes, there were ten inches of insulation plus soundproofing up there and if a bomb dropped He wouldn't hear it.

"Oh, my dear Chawz," said the Professor, "as we know, if it were only a simple matter of bombs, my dear fellow." And then he gave a lecture on the future of the world that wasn't much cheerier than Mrs. Lamb's. He ended up by saying, "Well, Chawz, I only hope my work will be remembered, as I know yours will."

That did it. He beamed and was nice for the rest of the day. He loves flattery and I don't suppose that even learning that the Professor is a dirty old man would spoil the Professor's image.

He took the Professor out to a posh restaurant for dinner. Needless to say, we were not invited.

Of such is the warp and the woof of our timeless existence.

Isn't that a neat sentence? I got it out of a book.

For a week now I have been praying very hard, every night. On my knees. So far I have had absolutely no results, which is not surprising, I guess, since I'm never sure who I'm addressing. I seem to get God and The Holy Spirit and Jesus all mixed up, like the Marx brothers.

And it's no comfort that my prayers may not be answered

how or when I want, like Mrs. Lamb says, because I want them answered now. My mother has been sick long enough and it's not fair.

There's so much I don't know. Such as, even if there *is* a God, which I'm still not sure of, does He answer small requests or does He just handle big business? After all, I'm not asking for any deal like raising Lazarus from the dead, like Mrs. Lamb told me about. I don't even ask to be saved when the day of resurrection comes. I just want my mother to get better.

I asked my father about God and Jesus and the Bible. "Don't ask me. Just read the fine print and don't sign anything," was all He said.

As if I wouldn't read the fine print. Especially if He wrote it. Honestly, you wouldn't believe it, but last year Marian came home from school in tears. They had sent out some sort of questionnaire for parents to fill out and opposite "Occupation" He had written "Swineherd." Then He crossed that out and wrote, "I mean Drunkherd."

The teacher thought it was a riot and read it out loud to the class. Poor old Fatso has been known as Marian McDrunkherd ever since.

Fortunately I am adopted and not related to these people.

Marian was so mad she wouldn't speak to Him for five days. I must admit I admired her because it takes guts to do that to Him. I can't stay mad for long, but Marian could keep it up forever if she felt like it.

Every time He spoke to her she just gave Him this long, icy stare. He tried everything, including joking and bullying but it didn't work.

He has never, in His entire life, been known to say that He

is sorry. Instead, He gives you money. Which, considering He is the stingiest (and, He says, poorest) person in the whole world, isn't such a bad idea.

Well, Marian wouldn't take his money. She just shoved it right back across the table, her mouth real mean-looking.

Finally, on the fifth day, she got a registered letter delivered at the door. In it was a ten-dollar bill and a note signed, "A devoted admirer, Charles McDumb."

She finally laughed, but no one will ever have to tell either of us to read the fine print.

Well, anyhow, back to Mrs. Lamb's pamphlets. I showed them to Him because Fatso made me a dare and said He wouldn't let me read them if He knew. She says it's a lot of baloney when He says there will never be any censorship in his house and we can read anything we like.

I won. He looked at it and said, "My dear child, if you want to read this garbage, be it on your own conscience. But please, publish it in the streets of Ashkelon that your poor old daddy did not force it on you."

"Do you think it will help?" I asked.

"Help what?"

"Well, anything," I said. Naturally I couldn't come out and say anything about my Mother. People never say what they really think, at least not in this house.

"Damned if I know," He said. "But nothing ventured, nothing gained. Just don't confuse this nonsense with the King James version of the Bible, which is the most magnificent book ever written."

Then he said something that really surprised me.

"I read it constantly, you know. Oh, the majesty of it! Isabel—Listen to this!"

Then He recited something about charity. It was really very beautiful. All I can remember is, "Though I speak with the tongues of men and of angels, and have not charity, I am become as sounding brass," and something about seeing through a glass, darkly.

"Did you like that?" He asked. When I said yes, He said He would type it out for me and I could memorize it.

I don't think I understand the King James version of the Bible, but one thing is clear. It's sure a lot better writing than Mrs. Lamb's pamphlets.

The day before yesterday Miss Swanson called me into her room after English class.

She said, "You know, Isabel, you told me you wanted to be a writer and I have great hopes for you."

I was really beginning to feel good when she said,

"Therefore, dear, I must ask you why every other word in this story you have turned in is that particular four-letter obscenity?"

I was genuinely puzzled. I thought that's what people wanted to hear. Also, that's what all the real writers do, and even in the movies. So I said, "He says it in *The Catcher in the Rye,* and that's on our required reading. It's so my readers will know how upset my characters are."

She said, "I think Mr. Salinger had something more in mind." Then she sighed and took off her glasses and said, "Come here, child."

I stood beside her and she put her arm around my waist and said, "Isabel, it has been overworked and shows a dearth of literary expression. You must learn to write so that your readers understand your characters' feelings without falling back on such banalities, for that's all words such as that are.

They betray the writer's inability to express himself."

As I stood there thinking, she said, "I have great faith in you, dear. Someday you will achieve your goal. I will be so proud. And think how proud your father will be, too."

She's got this crazy idea He's some jolly old daddy who just adores me. The truth of the matter is He doesn't like anybody, kids in general and his own in particular. He's good to my mother most of the time, except He won't make her face the facts about Bud.

"Be like him, Isabel! Be like your father! Be yourself!"

That didn't make much sense, but there was no point in trying to explain it to outsiders, so I just smiled. I'm an awful hypocrite.

"Be yourself, Isabel! Be your own woman! Never join the mob, Isabel, never join the mob! Promise me! I have great faith in you, Isabel."

So I promised. She is such a wonderful person I would do anything to please her.

I said, "It will be easy to take the words out of the story, but what will I put in, instead?"

Miss Swanson smiled.

"You must not do it to please me, dear. What will you put in? Ah, there's the rub. That's what makes the difference between being a writer and just writing. It all has to come from your head and no one can help you. You have chosen the most difficult of all professions, Isabel."

Then she stood up and brushed the hair off my forehead.

"Promise me you will *never* join the mob, Isabel."

So I promised again. It's one that shouldn't be hard to keep. No matter how hard I try, I'm always on the outside, looking in. The Little Match Girl, that's me. But it's nice to do anything that pleases Miss Swanson. Next to my mother and my sister-in-law Bonnie and Conn O'Rourke—who is three years older than me and in Old Fatso's class—I love Miss Swanson more than anybody.

She is between thirty and forty, plump, with eyes just like Peggy's. I wish all my teachers were like her. I get straight A's in English. If Mr. Cooper-Smythe, my Latin teacher, were like her, I'll bet I could even get A's in that class.

Beeyatreechee used to be Miss Swanson's best pupil, but now I am. I know Beeyatreechee is jealous because right in front of Naomi Schinbein and Debbie Stevens she said I sucked up to Miss Swanson. Beeyatreechee's father is the Anglican minister and since everybody's parents in this snobby community want to be up in the Anglican church, Beeyatreechee carries a lot of wallop.

Well, not everybody, of course. Naomi Schinbein and her sister Rhea are Jewish and Conn O'Rourke goes to the Catholic church. We don't go anywhere. I wish we did. It's no fun not belonging to *anything*.

Last year I asked if I could become a Catholic. Old Fatso said, "Ha, ha. You just want to go to Mass so you can see Conn O'Rourke."

"You shut up!" I yelled and He yelled "Both of you shut up. And you, no, you can't become a Catholic. Anything Old Mother Serpent can teach you, I can, and right here at home."

Whatever that means. Anyway, I get the drift of it, which is that I can't become a Catholic.

Yesterday, on one of the rare occasions when Fatso and I were speaking, I said I'd become a Catholic when I grew up and she said, no, I couldn't. I said I would so and she said I couldn't ever.

"Why?" I asked. Gee, maybe I was really Jewish and not related to these crummy Irish at all.

"Because I went through the big desk in the den and I found our birth certificates, Bud's, mine and yours, and we were all baptized Catholics when we were two weeks old. He and Mumma on their marriage certificate are both listed as Catholics. And once you're *baptized* a Catholic, you are one. I read it in Ann Landers, so it must be true. You can't unbaptize yourself; so you can't become one—because you already are."

This house is riddled with secrets.

"I am going to ask him why He never told us," I said.

"Don't you dare!" shrieked Marian. "He'll know I've gone through the big desk. I'll kill you if you say one word!"

I said I thought the big desk was always locked and she said it was but when He flew to the States and He'd been getting his papers and was in a hurry, He left the key right out on top.

"What else was in there?" I asked.

"A bunch of newspaper stories about Bud being killed and insurance policies and wills and stuff like that. *Time* magazine called Bud 'That misguided, unfortunate young Canadian.' "

I sat wondering why He hates Catholics so much. Of course, He hates everything else, so I suppose there's no reason to leave them out.

His only religion is his work, his nutty old cybernetics, which is the study of computers, their effect on people, and what they will do to and for us in the future.

"You'll never guess what else I found," Marian said. "Some reports from the school on our IQs. Bud's wasn't there. Just yours and mine."

Hers said that while they could not disclose her IQ, it was in excess of 150 and they wished her parents' consent to do a follow-up study on her till the university level.

"What did mine say?" I asked.

Well, wouldn't you know it. Mine said that while my intelligence was within the normal range, my attention span was limited.

Now this is arrant nonsense, as He would say. Why, only yesterday, in math class, I was accused of that very thing. The point, which nobody but me has ever grasped, is that I don't think of things at the same time as other people. For instance, yesterday, while everybody else was still thinking about square roots, I was thinking about shooting fish in a barrel. You see, the night before, on TV a guy said something was as easy as shooting fish in a barrel. This worries me considerably, as it doesn't make sense.

I mean, first of all, if you go shooting into a barrel filled with water, you're soon going to have a problem on your hands with both holes and water. And suppose you go and get yourself a steel barrel. Well, you are in a worse pickle because if you stop to use your head you would realize the bullets can ricochet and are just as likely to kill you as any fish. And finally, I don't care how dumb fish may be, no fish is so dumb as to just stop swimming and wait to be shot. As a matter of fact, I saw on a Jacques Costeau show that fish *have* to keep swimming or they drown.

I explained all this to Fats and you know what she said?

She said that's just another example of attention span. There we are discussing our IQs and I start talking about fish in a barrel.

Today was an almost May Spoonish day, lovely and sunny with whitecaps skimming all over the bay and the sky a startling blue. I decided to stop over at the Colonel's for a game.

20

Nobody knows much about the Colonel, although he has lived here for years and years. As a matter of fact, a lot of people don't know much about a lot of people in West Vancouver. As my father says, it's one of the few places where people know how to mind their own goddamn business, which is why we live here, I guess.

For instance, Sarah Peabody, whose house is in a very swank area called Chartwell, lived next door to a very quiet couple who traveled a lot. Once, Mrs. Peabody went next door to use the phone when theirs was out of order. The lady, who she met for the first time, told her that her husband was a traveling salesman and they owned a yacht and his hobby was helicopter piloting.

One day the Mounties came and took the man and the lady away. He was a traveling salesman, all right. He was head of one of the biggest, most elite heroin-smuggling circles in the world. Sarah said that after living next door to him for two years, she couldn't even remember what he looked like, he was so ordinary.

Not that there's anything sinister about the Colonel, except maybe his tendency to have tantrums. Retired Army, of course. West Vancouver is full of retired generals, air marshals, and admirals. One man who delighted my father got his name in the paper because he put Leading Aircraftsman R. Gifford Ret., on his mail box.

I've known the Colonel since I was just a kid and it seems that it was only yesterday when we met. I was riding past his fence on my bike when suddenly this beautiful scent hit me. It was like sticking your face into a bunch of flowers and it reminded me of something I've almost forgotten. Isn't it funny how smells can do that? I've often noticed it.

I got off my bike and leaned over the fence. What I smelled was roses. Cinnamon toast. A rubber hot-water bottle. Pitch in burning logs in the fireplace. The first day of a new year at school and the oil they clean the desks with and fresh chalk. Frying onions at the Fair. Smoking wax candles at birthday parties.

I sniffed and sniffed the roses. It was like those memories that the May Spoon never quite brings back. Someday when I'm feeling very very personal, I'll explain about the May Spoon. It's a rather holy thing and one that you can't go nattering about any time. Besides, it's magic and you have to be careful about magic. If you talk about it, it may go away.

I could have stood there with my head between the iron palings of the Colonel's fence forever, but something hard and cold grabbed the back of my neck. It was the crook of the Colonel's walking stick and he was on the other end of it.

Everybody around here has heard of the Colonel. He's a mean old bugger, if you will pardon the expression.

Anyhow, he bellowed, "What do you think you are doing! Get away from my fence!"

I said I couldn't with his cane wrapped around my neck. I said I wasn't doing any harm.

He said, "What right do you have to go around smelling other people's roses? Who the hell do you think you are?"

I might as well say right now this is no Shirley Temple story. The Colonel is as mean today as he was then. It's just that now he trusts me.

I said to the Colonel that his garden smelled different from other gardens, that it reminded me of something, but I couldn't remember what.

He let go of my neck and leaned over the fence. He stared at me for a long time, then said,

"Then don't remember. It is better to forget. Far better."

Well, my mother has forgotten, and I know it isn't better, so I told him some things are good to remember.

22

The Colonel stood twirling his waxed white moustache ends, his bushy brown-and-gray eyebrows meeting over his big beaked nose. He stands so straight you would think, if you didn't know him, that he had back trouble.

Finally he said, "So you like flowers?"

I said yes, we didn't have any of our own except for just a few tatty old things that came up on their own every year around the house, since neither of my parents cared about gardening.

He then invited me in to his garden to see all his flowers.

The two Misses Pettigrew, who live next door, were whispering and poking each other. They're a couple of nosey old biddies and the Colonel made a horrible face at them, so I did, too. I'd wanted to for years.

Mrs. Pettigrew is a widow and Miss Pettigrew is Mrs. Pettigrew's husband's sister. Miss Pettigrew cuts her hair short and wears tweeds and Mrs. Pettigrew has a mouth bigger than the Grand Canyon.

The Colonel specializes in roses. It seems he is famous in rose circles and his garden is a fairyland. It wouldn't have surprised me to see real fairies skipping down the garden paths.

Oh, the flowers! Great clumps of them everywhere! Yellow and pink irises which I always thought just came in plain old blue, and big pink carnations edged with scarlet, smelling like one of my favorite smells, cinnamon toast, and big, bold, sharp, bright flowers that look like spears, and believe it or not, are called red-hot pokers. There are patches of daphne you would think were singing until you realize it's the bees swarming over them. The paths are bordered by checkered ribbons of blue and white alyssum and lobelia and stocks and wallflowers. And among all these are marigolds, which look pretty enough until you smell them. They stink.

The Colonel told me the names of all his flowers, and then confided that his greatest ambition is to grow a black rose. No one has ever done that but he thinks he can through secret methods he has devised which people are trying to find out from him, but they won't, because he is wise to them.

He has invented quite a few roses and named them, which you are allowed to do if you invent one.

He showed me The Montgomery Gore, which is named after General Montgomery and is blood-red. The Eisenhower Snot is a dirty mustard color. The Colonel does not like General Eisenhower. He calls him that little Yank Bounder. The Zhukov Doom is a pale rose-color with a sort of sinister purplish glow from the center. The Katushka is the reddest red you ever saw and the Jap Flame Thrower is white, tinged with bright yellow and orange. The Samurai is a funny, irregular shape and the color is hard to describe, a pink with dark maroon lines in it. Then there's Tenno, The Emperor, pure white with a butter-yellow center. Alexander's Tunis is the color of sand with blood spilled on it. Everything seems to be blood or fire.

I said they were kind of funny names and he said, "By their names ye shall know them."

The Colonel has a large German shepherd dog called Rommel, who is also mean. Rommel snarled at me.

"He's very big," I said. "How much does he weigh?"

"Nine stone," said the Colonel.

"What's a stone?" I asked.

"Fourteen pounds. Can you figure that out?"

I said to myself, ten times fourteen is one hundred and forty, minus fourteen makes one hundred and twenty-six.

"Gee," I said. "He weighs thirty-eight pounds more than me!"

That was ages ago, of course. Now he only weighs twenty-nine pounds more than me.

The Colonel called Rommel over and told me to shake hands with him.

Well, I'm stupid but I'm not crazy. I backed away and said no.

Then the Colonel said a strange thing.

"If you want to come back again, you can. It gets lonely here. No one to play games with, so if you want to come back you can. Do you want to?"

I thought for a moment and decided I would like to live in this beautiful garden for the rest of my life. I said yes.

Then he said, "Rommel will savage anyone who doesn't know the password. As long as you know the password, you are safe. You must lean down and whisper in his ear, 'Kill Carruthers.'"

Rommel has a mouthful of teeth like sharpened piano keys and I wasn't going to lean anywhere near him.

"It's all right," said the Colonel. "I am holding him. Just whisper in his ear."

So, I took a deep breath and whispered, "Kill Carruthers."

Rommel suddenly wagged his tail, his ears flapped down and he sat on his haunches.

"Go on, girl," said the Colonel "Shake hands with him. Go on, stick out your paw."

So I did and Rommel stuck out his and we shook hands.

The Colonel asked me my name and when I told him he asked if I was McMurry, that cybernetics man's daughter. When I said I was he said, "Well, well. I hear he's an eccentric. A clever eccentric. Are you clever, girl?"

I said no, as a matter of fact I was kind of stupid. He said well, he expected I would catch on to some of his games without too much trouble. Then he asked me if I would like to go to his house and play a game with him.

"What kind of game?" I asked.

"We'll start with an easy one," he said, and to make a long story short, we've been playing games ever since.

The Misses Pettigrew phoned my father and said they saw me going into the Colonel's house. He told them to mind their own damned business and He said to me later, "I hear he is an eccentric. I would like to meet him. Ask him to drop over some time."

Now, if you knew how many people *drop* over to our house, you'd see the funniness of all this, because the same goes for the Colonel.

I said I'd ask.

Fatso, of course, said everybody knew the Colonel was crazy and people would talk but He just said I could probably find worse companions.

The next time I went the Colonel showed me how to unlock the very complicated set of combination locks on the front gate. Then I whispered the password to Rommel and he wagged his tail and shook my hand.

After that the Colonel and I had to go through this ritual of making sure Carruthers wasn't around. You have to be awfully careful about Carruthers. The only place he can't get into is the big billiard room downstairs where we play most of our games. I don't know why he can't get in there. The Colonel says it's like Switzerland; neutral and out-of-bounds.

I have never seen Carruthers, but I know what he looks

like. The Colonel showed me a picture of him so I'd recognize him.

Carruthers is tall and very good-looking, with a mustache. He's young and he's wearing funny army clothes with short pants. Desert gear, the Colonel says.

The Colonel is not a Colonel at all. He is really a General and he's a Lord, the son of an Earl. But he's living incognito, which means pretending to be somebody else, because of Carruthers.

He said he regrets that he will be unable to accept my father's kind invitation.

Today I was thinking about the May Spoon. The May Spoon was a very, very old spoon that Marian and I found in the garden when we were very little. It is a magic spoon. I never heard of any one having a magic spoon before, but we found it on a magic day. We were digging in the garden with little kids' shovels, eating raspberries from the bushes, everything smelling as beautiful as the Colonel's garden, and there it was. On the ground, dull but shining, almost invisible but gleaming. And real. A magic spoon and a magic moment.

Today I asked my father about it, and to my utter amazement, he understood right away.

He says that once in a lifetime everybody experiences an inexplicable moment of beauty and most people spend the rest of their lives wondering what brought it about.

"It is magic, isn't it?" I asked.

He shrugged. "That's one word for it, I suppose. The medieval saints called it illumination."

"Is there any way I can get illuminated again?"

"Some saints have. But obviously that precludes you. Now you take Saint Teresa of Ávila, for instance, a tough old bunny if ever there was one. She was a real humdinger at finding magic May Spoon moments. Saint Francis was no slouch either. Of course, you have to understand that they spent a hell of a lot of time praying."

"I tried that and it doesn't work."

He ruffled my hair. "Keep trying. Maybe you'll hit it lucky. Some guy in Toronto won the million-dollar Lotto twice, so miracles do happen."

About six months ago I was taking Peggy for a walk along the beach. It's beautiful there. It's straight down the hill, about a quarter of a mile from our house. You walk along the edge of the beach and if you turn around you see the big North Shore mountains going up and up and up, just a mile away. In the winter they're so white with snow it hurts your eyes to stare at them and in the summer they're the color of blue smoke. Behind them are two big peaks called The Lions, which are supposed to guard the harbor. I don't think there is another place in the world where you can see the ocean and the mountains so close at the same time.

When I was little I used to wonder what was behind the mountains. I asked my father and he told me, "More mountains." I didn't believe him.

Last year our whole class went on a fifteen-minute flight in an airplane around the city, the Gulf Islands, and the mountains. It was just like He said. Behind our mountains are hundreds of miles of big jagged ridges that don't look any more real than those relief maps you see in a museum.

Anyway, I was down at the beach, throwing a stick for Peggy and picking it up before she could because her arthritis in her hips is so bad she can hardly run, when I saw them.

A bunch of trucks were dumping rocks and fill all along our beach. The next day when Peggy and I went back there were a lot of men with drills breaking the rocks, and more trucks.

Finally I got enough nerve up to go and ask one of the men what was happening.

He was a young Italian, and their foreman. He grinned and said don't I ever read the newspapers. Then he said there's going to be the Centennial seawalk project all along here, and there's not going to be any beach. They are going to fill it all in with rock and then build this cut stone sidewalk and wall, all the way from here to Ambleside.

Well, you could have knocked me over with a feather. What a terrible thing to do!

I said, "But why do they want to fill the beach in with rocks?"

He said to protect the wall. Otherwise the big waves in winter would come right up here with logs and pound down the new wall.

I could have cried. I've been walking along this beach ever since I *could* walk. Where are the little kids going to build sand castles and hunt for baby crabs and wade and everything? You can't get near the water now without breaking a leg wherever they've worked and dumped the rocks. Already they have done about five blocks and every day people get all dolled up to come and stroll up and down. Everybody says it's just like the Promenade Anglaise or something in Nice. One of the worst things is there are big signs saying "No Dogs."

I still walk where the men are not working. There are no signs there. They are working from here to Ambleside and when they get to Ambleside then they'll come back here and start working on the other side. When it's finished it will be one long sidewalk several miles long.

It just makes me sick, absolutely sick. Why do people have to go changing things? What was the matter with a nice ordinary beach with clams and seaweed and mussels? At Ambleside there's a park with signs everywhere saying don't do this and don't do that and no parking and no overnight camping and no drinking parties permitted, no bicycling, and dogs must be leashed. There are phony playgrounds with swings and tunnels made of big sewer pipes and a concession that sells fish and chips and hot dogs. It's just simply horrible and soon Dundarave will be the same way.

I keep about three blocks away, on the good side, from the men, but they have got used to me when I pass and give Peggy bits of sausage. They are all Italians and He says they are masons from a special part of Italy. I asked Him at dinner if there wasn't any way we could stop them but He says I should have shouldered my community duties earlier and have picketed the local council meeting when it passed the resolution a year ago.

For crying out loud, how could I? I didn't even know it was going to happen so then He said that's no excuse, that's how the Nazis came to power, although I don't see any connection.

Oh, if only things would stay the way they were and quit changing. She wouldn't be the way She is if things hadn't changed and who knows, maybe even He wouldn't, although Bonnie, my sister-in-law, who meets me after school sometimes and takes me for a drive, says He was a mean son-of-a-bitch long before it all happened anyway. She says He used to beat hell out of Bud when he was a kid if he didn't do exactly

30

what he was told, and that they never stopped fighting about one thing or another from the time Bud was fifteen.

She ought to know. She lived with us then while Bud was with the Viet Cong. I never think about Bud.

Every day now I look up a new word in the dictionary and memorize it. It was Miss Swanson's idea and is sort of a sacred duty to me. Just pick it out at random, she says, and you will be amazed at what you will learn. He says it is no good unless I *use* the word the day I get it. Yesterday my word was cosignatory so I asked him if He and Her, I mean She, were cosignatory owners of the house. He said as a matter of fact they were. Today my word is arbitrary.

Arbitrary means decided or deciding according to judgment or will; independent of law or rule; discretionary; capricious; despotic. I looked *them* all up and they *all* mean different things.

It is very puzzling. I told old Fatso she was arbitrary since most of those words apply to her.

Tonight I got ten lines of Shakespeare to memorize for belting Fatso with the dishcloth because it *was* her turn to wash and there were loads of greasy, dirty, sticky pots and pans. But anyway, she got fifteen for hitting me back. He says she is older and it's time she started acting it. She must set an example for me. Ha, ha.

I wish He would quit picking that dumb *Timon of Athens* for me to memorize.

Last month he made a mistake and told me to memorize ten lines from *Titus Andronicus* instead of *Timon of Athens*. Wow! What a plot! I read the whole works through three times and I still didn't understand it. I mean, just how do you go about understanding a play where, in the last act at a big dinner, the main actor cooks up two meat pies with the bad guys in them and serves them to their mother? One of the girls got her hands cut off, got raped and had her tongue torn out and in the end everybody got killed off as usual in Shakespeare.

I bet I know more Shakespeare than any other kid in West Vancouver, although Bonnie says Bud must have set some kind of record.

Believe it or not, my friend Miss Swanson thinks this memorizing is a wonderful idea and would like to have it started in our school.

I told Fatso about this and she said if wanting to be a writer wasn't just another of my childish ideas, Miss Swanson might be right except that in her opinion there is no future in being a writer because we are the second generation to grow up with TV and by the time I learn how to write no one will know how to read.

This worried me considerably and I asked Miss Swanson about it. Miss Swanson said,

"I do hope she is not right, my dear. Oh, Isabel! To think that the youth of the future may never have the joys and sorrows of knowing Tom Sawyer or Catherine Earnshaw or Oliver Twist, or David Copperfield, or our own beloved Anne Frank. Oh, pray that she is wrong, my dear!"

Then she put her arm about my waist and squeezed me and said, "But then, Isabel, who knows? You may be a beacon, glowing, in time to come, your destiny to light the way for the feet of little lost children who are searching for more than a world such as Marian envisions. Isn't that a lovely thought, Isabel?"

Miss Swanson is the most wonderful person in the whole world.

I am sitting in my room, writing at my little desk. Many years ago this desk belonged to my mother's mother, Ann Carleon. Then my mother had it, then Bud, then Minnesota Fats, and now me. It is mahogany with lots of curlicues, a sloping top covered with ink-stained leather, and above that a hinged flat top that has places for ink, pens, and pencils when you lift up the lid. If you turn the pen place at a certain point, it revolves and you have a secret drawer. I keep my diary under the sloping part which has a lock, and I wear the key around my neck, the only safe place in this house.

I love this little desk and when They grow aged and die I am going to grab it before Old Fatso does. Ann Landers says that's how people get things after people die if you're not careful. I don't want anything else in this house but I want the desk, and if Fatso thinks I want it, then she'll want it and she's not going to get it. This house is full of antiques anyway, and she can have the rest.

Looking down at me from the wall of my bedroom with her sad, sad eyes, is a three-foot poster of the real Anne Frank. Next to her is an enlarged cutaway plan showing all the floors, including the attic, of their place in Amsterdam. Naomi Schinbein went there last year with her parents and saw the marks on the wall where the real Anne's father had marked her height, and pictures of the real Anne's favorite movie stars were still pinned up. When I am grown-up I will visit it. It will be a pilgrimage. I think about her a lot, especially when things are rotten around here. I imagine hearing the footsteps of the thief on the stairs, and then celebrating the Jewish Christmas, and finally, the very worst part, which she didn't get to write about: the Gestapo breaking down the door. Then I know that what I think is so terrible—how She is, and

Bud, and Fatso's meanness, and His temper—is not so bad. I think about Conn O'Rourke instead.

Anne Frank was just a bit older than I am now when she started her diary and I've read it so many times I know it almost by heart. Sometimes when things are really black I think it would almost be worthwhile living in that attic if I could have a father like hers and a sister who seem almost too good to be true.

He, of course, says my preoccupation with her is morbid and I ought to channel it into more healthful ways. He actually suggested, would you believe it, grass hockey. I would die before I would be caught dead playing such a dumb game. The girls at school who play it have legs like soccer players and I'd even rather be me than be like that.

Months and months until Christmas, which is about as happy as the workhouse around here anyway. I wish we had hordes of relatives like normal people. We have hardly anybody. Many years ago She had a sister called Auntie Madge who married and went to Australia. Auntie Madge got bit by a spider and died. I'll bet I'm the only person—besides Marian—in history to have an aunt die from a spider bite. Martha Koch had an aunt who hiccupped to death. That's pretty hard to beat.

He has a brother, Uncle Billy, living in Montreal. Uncle Billy is married to Aunt Ada and they have two grown-up sons called Barney and Dietrich. Uncle Billy and Aunt Ada came out to visit us about four years ago. He and Uncle Billy got into an argument about freight rates and they haven't spoken since. Don't ask me what it's all about. I don't even know what freight rates *are.*

Marian writes to Aunt Ada all the time, and sends Christmas cards from us to them every year, which makes Him furious. He says He wants no further truck with that drunken Irish swine. He means Uncle Billy, of course, not Aunt Ada. Aunt Ada, who is of German origin, sends us nice gifts every Christmas and on our birthdays and writes to us every month. She calls us her two motherless girls, which isn't correct because I have a mother.

Last year Aunt Ada sent Marian a beautiful necklace called a lavalier, which had belonged to His and Uncle Billy's mother. Aunt Ada sent it because she has no daughters. He was furious. Not that she sent it, but that Uncle Billy had had it all those years and He didn't know about it. He said it's just the sort of thing you could expect from that drunken Irish swine. It seems a priest gave it to Uncle Billy just after their mother died. She had asked the priest to give it to the first son who arrived at her deathbed.

When Uncle Billy and Aunt Ada came out from Montreal He and Uncle Billy hadn't seen each other for years and years. Aunt Ada says that it seems almost impossible that they are brothers and share the same genes because they are so different. My father is successful and hardworking and sober, she says, and Uncle Billy is drunken and lazy and irresponsible. Well, that's what she says, not me. Actually they look very much alike, although she can't see it. Uncle Billy has black curly hair and He has blonde, straight hair. Uncle Billy is fat and He is thin. But they are the same height and have the same complexion. Their faces are very similar, although Uncle Billy once got his nose broken in a fight and it's sort of lopsided. Aunt Ada wants Uncle Billy to have plastic surgery, but he's already had so much surgery that he's had just about everything you can have out taken out. Aunt Ada is a real stickler for health and looking after yourself. Uncle Billy says she can just leave his face alone, it gives him character, otherwise he'd look too much like Charlie (my father).

Uncle Billy and He had had a fight years and years before the freight-rates one. Neither of them could remember what the original fight was about; all they could remember was that they didn't like each other. Compared to them, Marian and I are the Bobbsey Twins.

Uncle Billy used to own a fancy restaurant and bar and was rich, but Aunt Ada says he was his own best customer and that's how he lost it. Now he's a postman and Aunt Ada, who is a nurse, is night matron of a hospital in Montreal. Barney graduated from McGill, but Dietrich dropped out in his first year and Uncle Billy says he is a Communist bum. My father says that being a bum is one of the occupational hazards of being related to Uncle Billy.

All of my grandparents were dead before I was born. I think I'll have a lot of kids when I grow up so they won't be lonely. As long as they're not like old Fatso. Or me.

It's funny; you really never know about people. When Marian was visiting back east with Aunt Ada and Uncle Billy, Aunt Ada used to tell her stories about when she was first married to Uncle Billy, and about her family and Uncle Billy's, which, of course, is ours, too.

My Father has never mentioned His family. As far as we know from Him He could have dropped from outer space. Who knows? Maybe He did.

Aunt Ada says that actually it is all really rather sad and explains a lot about each of the brothers, especially one aspect of Uncle Billy.

Their father had what Marian says Aunt Ada refers to rather delicately as "a drinking problem."

There were four children, the two boys and two younger girls and one day the father, who I might as well refer to as my grandfather, because that's what he was, didn't come home.

They were poor to begin with but as you can imagine, this did not help matters much. My grandmother got a job in a cloth mill.

My grandfather had a lot of rich relatives in the States. In her desperation my grandmother wrote to them, and one of them got the two boys enrolled in a Jesuit boy's college as charity students. They hated it, and when they were thirteen and fifteen (Uncle Billy was older) they ran away, back to my grandmother.

She was having a very tough time making ends meet as it was, and couldn't support two extra mouths. As a matter of fact, she was so poor that the mill manager let her take imperfect bits of cloth and mill ends home and in the evening she used these to make beautiful children's clothes which she sold, and with the leftover scraps she made patchwork quilts.

So, the upshot was that it was all she could do to look after the two little girls, who were six and nine years old, and the boys had to leave and get work.

At first they got jobs in the town where she lived, but then those gave out, so they moved on, together. Not because they liked each other, because even then they didn't, but because they had no one else.

One day my grandmother received a letter from a woman in Montana who owned a ranch there. One of this woman's ranch hands had been thrown from his horse and had broken his neck.

Among his possessions this lady found a gold watch and a letter addressed to my grandmother. The lady opened the letter, she said, because she had no idea who he was. He hadn't been using the name of McMurry, but was known as Mahoney, which was his middle name. The watch had been his father's and was from Ireland.

The boys left town and worked in hotels, resorts, logging camps, construction groups—anything they could get. Fortunately, they were both as strong as oxes.

At first the two of them sent money home regularly to their mother, but then it stopped. Uncle Billy spent his on booze, which made my father angry and for a little while He sent his share home, but then He said He wouldn't unless Uncle Billy did, too, and He spent His money on books and correspondence courses. The result was that soon neither of them were helping her.

They split up, one going east and one west. Then, a year or so later, my father got a letter from His mother's priest, telling Him to come home immediately. He did, and when He got there, Uncle Billy was there, too. It was then that Uncle Billy got the lavalier, which He didn't find out about until years and years later, when Aunt Ada gave it to Marian.

Their two little sisters had died of tuberculosis several months before, and my grandmother died the day before Uncle Billy arrived and two days before my father did.

The priest told them their mother had died of a broken heart, which, as Marian says, must have made them feel just dandy.

As a matter of fact, their mother also died of tuberculosis, which the priest knew, Aunt Ada says.

Well, they left, and it was then that my father embarked on His education program. Every cent he made He saved for tuition and school and university. Aunt Ada says there was no stopping Him, any more than anyone could stop Uncle Billy from drinking.

He worked all the time He was going to university and He took every degree there was. Finally He had all the degrees He wanted in this country, so He went to England and took some more. He came back to Canada, met my mother, and married her.

Uncle Billy's career was similar, but in a different direction. They were like two lines, says Marian, that met at one common point and then flared out in opposite ways.

After their mother died, Uncle Billy worked just as hard as my father, also with only one view in mind: buying land.

All he thought about was buying property, building on it, and selling it for a profit. When he was twenty-two he was a millionaire. He bought, among other things, a hotel with a bar where he used to sit with his business cronies and drink. By the time Uncle Billy was thirty, he was broke. And a drunk.

Aunt Ada had married him because she thought she could save him. Rehabilitate is the word Marian uses. Well, she couldn't. He didn't give a damn about money or staying sober or anything else.

Aunt Ada says it is quite obvious both brothers are riddled with guilt.

Marian says one is allergic to booze and the other to books.

Strangely enough, Uncle Billy has always adored his boys. Marian says that he may kid them and call Dietrich a bum, but he has never laid a hand on them and they worship him.

Another strange thing. Even Uncle Billy rarely mentions his father, mother, or little sisters. All Aunt Ada knows is what Uncle Billy has said when he is drunk, and she says that considering how much he drinks, even that is precious little.

Aunt Ada says the Irish are like that. She says you think they tell you a lot because they talk so much, but they tell you just what they want you to know. She says it's different when they're angry and sober. They let you know what they think then, although a lot of the time they pretend they're joking.

I really don't think Aunt Ada understands the Irish.

Aunt Ada made Marian promise and swear to die never to tell anyone but me all about this. She said Uncle Billy would never forgive her. I wouldn't have thought that by this time she still cares, but apparently she does.

So, my grandfather is buried in a pauper's grave on the outskirts of a little cowboy town in Montana and my grandmother in a Catholic cemetery on the edge of a little town in Ontario.

Marian is very interested in genealogy, which is the study of your family. It's tough in our case. Marian says that trying to find out anything about our mother's family was ten times harder than His, because my mother is the last of them.

Everything Marian learned came from Aunt Ada, but Aunt Ada didn't meet our mother until both had been married several months, and, as Aunt Ada put it, by that time they both had enough problems that they had more things to do than sit around and talk family.

All Aunt Ada could remember was that my mother's family, like His, were from Ireland, that they were Catholic, and that they were as poor as His. My mother had one sister, Auntie Madge, who, as I told you about earlier, went to Australia and died from a spider bite. Aunt Ada didn't think Auntie Madge had any children. Both my mother's parents were dead when Aunt Ada met her.

My mother had been a milliner when she met my Father. She was very beautiful and worked in this fancy shop that made hats to order for rich ladies. Aunt Ada says my mother had a real flair and was very original and artistic. Of course, as Aunt Ada says, women don't wear hats the way they used to.

Aunt Ada, who is a very fine seamstress herself and even

40

makes the boys' shirts, said she can't understand why Marian and I are so impossibly klutzy when it comes to sewing because both our mother and father's mother were beautiful needlewomen.

Aunt Ada has a needlepoint sampler made by my Grandmother Carleon when she was a child in Ireland, with her name and the date on it, which my mother gave Aunt Ada soon after they met. Aunt Ada was very fond of my mother. Still is, I guess.

Aunt Ada says I can have it when I grow up because Marian got the lavalier and Barney got the gold watch. I am going to get the little desk too, only they don't know about it. I don't know what Dietrich gets. Being a Communist, maybe he doesn't want any worldly goods, if it works that way.

So. There it is. My family history.

Yesterday, when I came out of school, my sister-in-law, Bonnie's old car was parked away down the block, under the chestnut tree where she always waits for me. I hadn't seen her for ages and let out a whoop and ran all the way. She said, "Hi, kiddo. Shut the door," as I bounced in beside her. We drove down to where you can park and see the ocean at Ambleside and I said,

"Gee, I thought you had forgotten I was alive, it's been so long!"

She smiled. "Sorry. I've been working nights as a cashier at a Greek dump on Broadway in Vancouver and I don't get through till one-thirty, so I seem to sleep most of the day."

She put her arm around me and I snuggled up next to her.

"Well, how's my favorite relative?"

"Fine," I said. "But I have a favor to ask."

"Shoot," she said.

"I want you to call me Ann. Ann, from now on. My full name is now Ann Carleon. It was my grandmother's name."

She shrugged, "Well, a rose by any other—"

"I didn't know you knew Shakespeare," I said.

"Oh, for God's sake, don't be such a damn pain in the ass like the rest of your family!"

I felt sort of hurt so she said, "Except your mother, of course."

That made it better and she said, "How is she, Isabel, I mean Ann?"

"Fine," I said.

"Nothing's changed?"

"Nothing."

She sighed. "Oh, well, you be good to her, Ann. You remember that. She was always good to me."

"I will," I said.

"How are you doing in school?"

"Fine. I got an A in English. I've got this really keen teacher called Miss Swanson this year. She says she thinks I'll be a really good writer if I ever learn the difference between it's and its."

Bonnie said that's nice.

"One's got an apostrophe," I explained.

"I know, for Christ's sake! Do you think I was brought up in Timbuktu or some place? Here, I brought you something."

It was a big chocolate bar.

"Be sure and brush your teeth when you get home."

I said thanks.

Somehow we always get around to the subject of Bud. Myself, I never think of him.

"Peggy still eating his dinner every night?"

I said yes, then told her about the beach and how they are changing it all the way to Dundarave.

"That'll take years," she said.

"Oh, yeah? You ought to see what they've done already. Why can't they leave things the way they were? Why do things always have to change?"

She squeezed me. "I used to wonder the same thing. I don't know, honey, but they always do. Bud and I used to walk on that beach every night when we were first married. They haven't torn down the pier, have they?"

"Not yet, but I suppose they will."

"He used to fish off it with one of those little two-bit wrap-around fish lines." She looked out the window. Then, "Damn him anyhow!"

I knew what was coming. She stubbed her cigarette and pushed me away.

"The stupid bastard! Why did he have to do that? He didn't even think of *me*! Can you believe it? All those Americans coming up here to dodge the draft and him a Canadian and perfectly safe, so what does he do? I'll tell you what he does! He goes down there and joins up and when he gets overseas to Vietnam the silly bugger transfers, voluntarily, just listen to this, transfers voluntarily, to the *wrong side*!"

"Well," I said, "I guess it wasn't the wrong side to him."

"They killed him for it, so it sure as hell wasn't the right side!"

She sighed and lit another cigarette. "I'm sorry, kiddo. I guess I'll never get over it. I have to let off steam sometimes. It's funny; you are the only one I can talk to about it. I wonder if it's because you look so much like him. Do you ever think of him, Isabel? I mean Ann?"

"No," I said.

"Well, you were just a little kid," she said and put her arm around me again. "Crazy bastard. There never was and never will be anybody like him again. If we'd had a little girl, she might be just like you except a few years younger. Say, how's Marian?"

"Old Fatso? As horrible as ever."

Bonnie laughed. "Oh, she'll probably outgrow it. Old Marian's not so bad. At your age sisters always fight. I used to fight with all of mine, and I had four of them."

I had just finished reading this marvelous book and I said, "The Brontës didn't."

"Oh? Where do they live? Are they new in the neighborhood? I don't remember you mentioning them before."

"No, I haven't," I said.

It was no use explaining. I couldn't share this wonderful book with Bonnie. There are some people you can't share some things with, especially books.

Now, old Fatso, for instance, would understand. Probably even Beeyatreechee would, and who knows, maybe even my father, only you can't count on Him for anything. But Bonnie, no.

It's too bad. I guess it works both ways. Sometimes Bonnie starts to say something to me then stops and says, oh, never mind, and I know it's one of those things she just can't be bothered trying to explain or spell out for me.

We sat quietly, watching the waves on the beach.

"Has your father still forbidden you to see me?"

I nodded.

Forbidden was hardly the word. He had said, "By God, if I ever find you hanging around that tramp I'll break every bone in your body."

He would, too. Marian was allowed to go to a party and had to be back at twelve. *Nobody* gets back at twelve these days. That went out with crinolines and bustles. Once she didn't get home until after one and He shouted, "I'm the head of this house and as long as you're under my roof you'll do exactly as I say, and if you don't like it get the hell out and don't come back." Then He slapped her face so hard her nose bled.

If I hit anybody that hard I'd be afraid I had hurt them but He had just said, "Next time I'll use my fist."

Bonnie said, "I'm fed up with working nights and I'm going to try and get a day job, so maybe I'll be able to see you more often. I'm glad you're doing so well in English and that you like Miss—Miss—what's her name?"

"Swanson," I said.

"Miss Swanson. How's your true love, Scarlett O'Hara, or whatever his name is?"

"It's Conn O'Rourke!"

"Sorry. I never was any good at names. Anyhow, how is he?"

"He still doesn't know I'm alive. Of course, I can understand why, with me being a hundred pounds underweight and absolutely hideous on top of that."

She got quite mad.

"Oh, shut up, you little nut. You're the spitting image of Bud. Do you think I'd go around marrying someone who was hideous? Quit talking about yourself that way."

"Well, I'm sure not beautiful," I said.

"You'll be all right." She cuddled me. "I'd better get you back before you're in trouble. There's nothing the matter with you that time won't cure. I know. I was like that myself."

"No kidding!"

"Sure. And look at me now. Believe me, every night guys proposition me. I could have married a dozen times over. Of course, I won't. But don't you worry. One of these days your legs and arms and hair and teeth will all fit together and you'll be a knockout."

I felt much better as I got out of the car.

"Hey, wait," she called me. "I've moved. I've got a new phone number." She gave me a piece of paper.

"You'd better memorize it and swallow it, like they do in spy stories, or your old man will find it."

I often call her by pay phone when I am blue. She says it cheers her up, too. Next to Mumma I love her best, even before Conn O'Rourke or Miss Swanson.

Last night He went to an antique auction. He is always going to them. As a matter of fact, having no friends through choice, as far as I can see, it's about the only time He goes out. Our house is filled with His antiques which He says He buys for their beauty and Marian says He buys for investments. I guess it's a combination of both, really, because He spends hours and hours dusting and polishing and gazing at them.

Rhea Schinbein, Naomi's older sister, came over and brought along this super girl, Jane Lonsdale, who is platinum blonde and very beautiful. She is just as nice as she is beautiful, and believe it or not, she is nineteen years old!

She is engaged to Rhea's brother, Fraser. I think Fraser Schinbein is a stupid name, although, I suppose if you sit down and think about it, it's no worse than Dietrich McMurry. Anyway, Dr. and Mrs. Schinbein are going out of their minds about Fraser marrying a girl who isn't Jewish. Rhea told Marian that in a Jewish family, particularly one with an only son, it is the very worst thing that can happen. I don't know what Jane sees in Fraser, whom I don't know, but have seen. He drives a Lamborghini sports car and Marian says he is into drugs. People are always talking about people being into drugs, but he's the only one I know of. I don't even know

46

where you get drugs. Nobody ever tries to sell *me* any. I would love to try pot; Marian says everybody at school uses it. Everyone except her. She says she doesn't care what anybody says, it dulls the mind. And boy, nobody and nothing is going to dull *her* mind. I asked her to get me some and she said are you kidding, stupid, you're dumb enough now.

Anyhow, Marian said let's make a ouija board, which she had read about, so we cleared the dining-room table and got out a cut-glass goblet and made slips of paper with the letters of the alphabet, which we put in a circle.

Oh, it was such fun! Marian asked if she would be the top student at school and it spelled out 'wong,' which at first we thought was a mistake, but then Marian remembered the Wong twins, who are her only competition and it was kind of scary.

Rhea asked how many children she would have and it said twenty-eight, and everybody howled when Marian said the spirits seemed to have it mixed up with her bra size.

Jane Lonsdale asked if she would win the Nobel Prize for Peace, and it said piece of what.

I asked my secret wish about Mumma and it kind of hemmed and hawed between yes and no. After that it got very skittish and finally Jane couldn't hold her laughter in any more and confessed she had been pushing it.

Then we tried raising a ghost by putting our hands on the table and concentrating. One end of the table *did* rise and scared the daylights out of me. When she saw how frightened I was, Rhea laughed and admitted she had been lifting the table with her knees.

Finally He came back, looking very pleased with himself, and made a beeline straight to Jane Lonsdale, ignoring Rhea Schinbein.

He strutted around, showing her an eighteenth-century

Japanese ladies' cosmetic box He had bought. It was black lacquer inlaid with silver. When Jane admired it He said He wanted her to keep it.

You could have knocked me and Marian over with a feather.

Jane laughed and refused, but kissed his cheek sort of playfully.

Marian and I exchanged unbelieving glances as He beamed at her. I for one thought He might belt her across the teeth.

Then, smiling happily, He took the cosmetic case upstairs. When He had gone I said I hoped it had Made In Japan stamped on the bottom.

Jane Lonsdale laughed even more, showing all her gorgeous teeth. She rumpled my hair and said I was a little beast. She said what a character He was and she wished we were her family.

Marian and I could hardly believe our ears.

"Whatever for?" asked Marian.

Jane said her father is a boring chartered accountant, her stepmother is a boring home-economics teacher, her brother is a boring corporate lawyer, and her sister is a boring physical-education nut. She said talk about Dullsville.

She is so much fun that I said maybe she was adopted like me and she laughed even more and said oh, how they could do with a few like me around their house. Marian said any time, day or night.

I asked Jane what she was going to be when she grew up and she said a lady of the evening and she bet our old man would be her first customer. Marian said don't say things like that in front of her, for God's sake, Jane. She takes everything literally and tells everybody everything.

I do not.

I don't know what a lady of the evening is and it isn't in the dictionary. Marian made me promise not to mention it and I said I wouldn't, but I'm going to ask Bonnie. Something's going on I don't understand.

It's funny; my adoptive family drives me nuts and I'd like to belong to Jane's and she wants to be one of us. Of course, she doesn't know what it's really like, but it goes to show you people are never satisfied.

I was kind of hoping maybe Jane would ask me over to meet her boring family but she didn't. I asked Marian if she would ask Jane over again and she gave me a funny look and said, honestly, you are not only dumb, you are retarded.

My word today is chagrin, meaning trouble or worry, also a feeling of vexation, disappointment, humiliation, or mortification.

Well, I could use that word seven days a week. Yesterday I took a story I wrote to Miss Swanson. I asked if I could stay after school and show it to her. It was a real neat story about this girl who was adopted by very commonplace people. During the course of her life it becomes apparent to her that she is very different and all the clues lead up to the fact that she is of noble birth.

Well, the punch line is that she wasn't adopted at all, as everybody who will read it thinks, but that she is a *reincarnation* (that means to be born again) of a princess.

Miss Swanson read it and said it was very good and showed imagination. Then she said,

"But Isabel, dear, don't you think the end is a bit contrived?"

Well, I don't know, I just don't. I mean, after all, show me a story that isn't. I didn't say that to her, though.

"How would you end it?" I asked, but she just laughed. She said that was the easy way out and it was *my* story.

"That's the beauty of being creative, Isabel. It's your very own. Incidentally, dear, your father never comes to the parent-teacher meetings, does he?"

"No."

"It would be nice if he would. Staff would love to meet him."

I gave my false smile and said I would tell Him.

Then she said, "Ask Him for me what he considers the most beautiful lines of poetry ever written in the English language."

Well, you'd think I'd know better after the swineherd affair, but at dinner I did ask. He wrote on a piece of paper and folded it and handed it to me. Fortunately I unfolded it and read it. I could have killed Him. It said,

> I put a slug in the slot machine,
> In the happy long ago.
> It seemed at the time
> More a lark than a crime.
> I was young, I didn't know.

I was furious. "That's not fair! You promised you wouldn't do things like that again and you know she's my favorite teacher!"

I began to cry. Not because I was sad but because I was mad. He is so vulgar. Thank heavens I am adopted.

He said, "Dry your tears, Melissande, dry your tears."

He took another piece of paper. This time he wrote, "Charmed magic casements opening on the foam/Of perilous seas in faery lands forlorn."

"I don't know what in hell it means but it should satisfy her romantic spinster's soul."

I took it to her today and she clasped it to her heart and said, "Oh, Isabel, you are so very lucky. How many young girls have fathers like yours?"

When I came out in the hall Beeyatreechee was there and she said, "You sure are trying to get in good with Miss Swanson, aren't you?"

I am not! I like Miss Swanson better than almost anyone. She always listens to me and encourages me to write, even if she isn't so good at judging the endings of stories.

Today Marian gave me the Indian sign, which is three fingers held up behind the head and means there is a letter from Aunt Ada.

As soon as He had gone to what Marian calls His lair, we rushed up to the box room, where we always go to read Aunt Ada's letters.

"Is there any money in it?" I asked. Aunt Ada usually puts in a five-dollar bill for us. He would have a fit if He knew. That's why we always hide in the box room to open her letters. There was five dollars in it, so I am now financially solvent for a while at least. He won't let me baby-sit, and Marian has only been allowed to for the last few months.

Aunt Ada has been asking for years for one of us to spend the summer with them in Montreal, but He always said no. Two years ago He changed His mind and let Marian go. She was there for seven weeks. She didn't say much about it when she got back, but in bits and pieces it's been coming out.

Aunt Ada is a nurse and the night matron of a hospital. She is very kind. She is also very thorough, something we aren't used to around here. Marian says our cousins Barney, age twenty-two, and Dietrich, age twenty-one, are almost never home, and Uncle Billy spends as much time as he can in bars. Although Marian is very fond of Aunt Ada, she says she really doesn't blame them. It seems Aunt Ada is a cleanliness and perfection nut. I don't mean like my mother, who will wash the kitchen floor twice in the same day because she can't remember doing it the first time. No, Aunt Ada means business. For instance, Fatso said, you have to turn your mattress *every* day. You have to put clean sheets and pillowcases on *every* day. If the mattresses get turned once a year around here it's news to me. Also, you have to chew each mouthful fifteen times because Aunt Ada says thirty percent of digestion takes place in the mouth.

She is very health-conscious, and Uncle Billy has had three operations: one for ulcers, one for his gall bladder, and one for bowel trouble. Aunt Ada says it is because of his drinking, but my Father says she just wants to find out what's inside Uncle Billy. He also says He could tell her without using surgery.

Marian says that such as home is, she would rather be here. I could go and visit Aunt Ada, but Marian says I would be sorry. I sure would love to see Montreal, but if Aunt Ada is as fussy as Marian says, I don't think I'd last very long.

Aunt Ada is a bundle of energy, which is rather odd because she is fat and I always think of energetic people as being thin. They have a very nice house with a big garden. Aunt Ada does all the gardening, and even mows the lawn. Marian says it's really something to see her out there with her straw hat on, digging in her vegetable garden like a coolie while Uncle Billy sits on the porch sipping beer. Aunt Ada not only grows all her own vegetables, she also cans and freezes them, and enters them in the provincial garden contests, which, of course, she wins. She also makes the boys' shirts, if you can believe that. She knits us sweaters, is an active member of the Lutheran church, and does a lot of work for them, such as making choir robes and baking.

She is a superb cook, although Marian says all the fun of eating is taken out by having to chomp endlessly.

And also, when you go to the bathroom there, you don't just wash your hands after. Everybody has their own little nail brush hanging up with their name on it. I asked Marian how Aunt Ada knew if you used it and Marian said she supposed Aunt Ada figured once she'd taught you you'd have the sense to do it on your own. I said I'd just wet the nail brush and hang it up again and she said you would. Aunt Ada does not believe in curtains or rugs as they collect germs, so Marian says their house is about as cosy as an institution.

Aunt Ada dearly wanted to adopt us after my mother got sick but He said He would sooner put kittens in a burlap sack and drop them in the handiest river as it would be a more merciful solution.

The really odd thing is that Aunt Ada does not hate Him the way He seems to hate her. He calls her "your Uncle Billy's Hun woman."

Aunt Ada does not hate Uncle Billy, Marian says. She just treats him as if he is sort of dumb, which Marian says he sure as hell isn't. She says it's his way of getting even at Aunt Ada. The whole thing is beyond me.

Marian says Aunt Ada is always raving about how wonderful and dependable and intelligent our father is. She, of course, does not have to live with Him.

Just the same, Marian says when Uncle Billy comes home from work with his feet swollen from walking all day being a postman, Aunt Ada always has a large basin of hot water and Epsom salts waiting for him.

Oh, yes. Aunt Ada irons *everything*. Even the towels and the boys' underwear. Since she is night matron of the hospital she doesn't get home until three o'clock, but she's always up at seven. She takes a nap at exactly two o'clock in the afternoon for exactly one hour and forty minutes. This seems to charge her up for another twenty-four hours.

It seems hard to believe with their upbringing, but Marian says both Barney and Dietrich are a couple of slobs. They expect to be waited on hand and foot, she says, never say thank you to Aunt Ada for anything, bolt their food just like we do, and bellyache if their freshly ironed shirts are not ready at the exact minute they want them. Aunt Ada also polishes their shoes, as well as Uncle Billy's. She told Marian that in her home the men were always the masters.

Maybe *that's* what's the matter with Uncle Billy.

Aunt Ada did not expect Marian to help with the house-work. Instead, she waited on Marian, too. She did let her dry the dishes and iron the tea towels, which Marian said she asked to do because she felt so guilty seeing Aunt Ada busy eighteen hours a day.

Aunt Ada doesn't read much, just the headlines of the papers, but Marian says she must be smart enough if she's matron. It certainly must be the cleanest hospital in the world, Marian says.

She told Marian all about the Emergency Ward and how dumb the doctors are, especially the young ones. Half the time she has to decide instantly what to do and make it look like the doctor's idea.

She told Marian to always beware, if she was suddenly taken to the hospital, never to have a resident physician from a foreign country look after her, because she might as well get a vet. Make sure they've been trained in Canada or the States, she says, and even then, have your own personal physician check up on *everything*. Aunt Ada says you wouldn't believe the blunders that would go unknown and unchecked if she weren't there.

I try to imagine the Emergency Ward with Aunt Ada in charge, and all I can see is her rushing about with a big white feather duster.

Oh, Lord. Now He's got this new half-baked idea that we have to read the paper and discuss current events at dinner, which is already enough to take your appetite away.

Minnesota Fats says it's my fault because all I ever read in the paper is Ann Landers and my horoscope.

Actually I like reading, but not the newspapers because it's always such lousy news. Every day it's revolutions, bombs, fires, earthquakes, famines, and/or assassinations.

A couple of weeks ago I read the best book I've ever read in my life, the one I wanted to tell Bonnie about. It is called *Wuthering Heights*, and Miss Swanson recommended it. She said she wished she were my age so she could read it again for the first time. I got it out of the library and I just couldn't put it down. At two o'clock in the morning He saw the light under my door and came in, furious. Then, when he saw what I was reading, He gave his "tee-hee-hee" laugh and said, "So you have finally discovered Withering Shites."

I was extremely disgusted and angry. He hardly ever says anything more than damn and hell and he didn't have to pick my favorite book to swear and even worse, joke about.

Miss Swanson said her sister, not Miss Swanson's but Emily Brontë's, wrote a book called *Jane Eyre* and I would probably love that, too. I tried to get it from the library but it was out.

Tonight, for news at dinner, I talked about the big flap there is in West Vancouver about cutting down trees so people can get a view of the water. The people with trees don't want a law passed and the people who live behind them do, which is logical enough.

Fatso said, "That's not important, stupid! It's supposed to be *international* news."

Then she started yapping about the Israeli-Arab situation and the Golan Heights and the Sinai desert as if she were Moses or somebody and He said,

"Excellent, Marian. You have a firm grasp of the facts. Now try and imagine yourself as an Arab, and when you are through that put yourself in the place of a Jew. Imagine yourself, as, say, your friend Rhea Schinbein."

Old Blabbermouth said, "Daddy, you know that's impossible. How could Rhea possibly be impartial and objective?"

"Very good, Marian, very good." Then he turned to me.

"I hope the Jews win," I said.

"You would," said Old Fatso. "That would mean a world war of course, wouldn't it, Daddy?"

I was thinking of the real Anne.

"That is not entirely a well-considered answer, Isabel, but at least you are honest and speak your own mind. And as a matter of fact, Marian, quite a lot of American and Canadian Jews are anti-Zionist and do not support Israel. But, I suspect, in their hearts there is always a gnawing anxiety."

I stuck my tongue out at Fats. I didn't think He'd see, but He did and said, "Do you wish to leave this table, young woman?"

Now, from the above conversation, you might think that we are a bunch of intellectuals who sit through our placid, lovely meals quietly discussing politics and coming up with thoughtful suggestions on how to run a better world. The truth of the matter is that we have these discussions when He feels like having them. If He's in a lousy mood or thinking about one of his kooky books, it's sit up straight, stop picking at that and eat it, and both of you shut up.

Well, as Bonnie keeps saying, that's life for you.

A week ago Beeyatreechee asked about ten of us to meet her on the stairs outside the gym at lunch hour.

She said, "My father has had the most wonderful idea. Daddy thinks we should form a club."

Nobody said anything. We just looked at each other. There was me, Beeyatreechee, Naomi Schinbein, Debbie Peters, Helen Henderson, Julie Black, Debbie Cunningham, Jill St. Lawrence, Jennie Fleming, and Martha Koch.

"What kind of a club?" asked Julie finally.

"A real one. We'll have a president and a secretary to take notes of the minutes, and dues, and, oh, lots of other things."

"Like what?" asked Helen.

"Whatever we want," said Beeyatreechee.

Helen said, "I know. We could go on hikes and take lunches, and go skiing in the winter."

And Jill said, "We've got a cabin on Mount Whistler. I bet my dad would let us stay overnight."

Everybody sat up and started looking interested.

"How much will the dues cost?" asked Naomi.

"Oh, not much. Just enough to cover small expenses."

"Can we have parties? I mean real ones, with boys?" asked Jennie.

"No," said Beeyatreechee, "it's not that sort of a club."

I was glad because I knew He wouldn't let me join if it were.

"But we'll have parties for us. Pajama parties, maybe."

"Gee, that sounds great," said Jennie. "Everybody could bring something to eat. You know, one person a cake, somebody else cookies and things like that."

Then everybody began having ideas.

We'd play tennis, go for hikes, go to Whistler, have garage sales, meet once a week, have seances and play with the ouija board, dance with each other, exchange records and make fudge. Oh, there were just hundreds of ideas.

Then somebody said, "Hey, let's have uniforms. Not really uniforms, but, like, jackets with the name of the club on them, so people will know who we are."

Everybody agreed on that and Naomi said, "My uncle owns a tailor shop. Maybe we could get the material cheap. I've heard him talk about things like getting too much that doesn't move. How much would we need each, Jennie? Two yards?"

Jennie is a super sewer and makes all her own clothes and looks like a junior model in them. "It depends on the width," Jennie said.

"We could make them ourselves," said Julie.

"We haven't got a sewing machine," I said.

"Oh, I'll make yours then. And I'll help anybody else who gets stuck," said Jennie.

It got superer and superer.

"And we'll put felt insignias with the name of our club on our jackets."

"What name?" said somebody.

Nobody knew so we all started thinking and we came up with real dumb things like the Glamour Girls, or Pussycats and the Heaven's Angels and things like that.

"None of those have got any class," said Naomi. "We need something unusual." She stopped and looked at me. "Isabel, why don't you ask your father? My father says that he must be a walking encyclopedia."

Little did she know it, but she had just solved the biggest problem for me. I wasn't at all sure He would let me join but if He has one weak spot it's that He just loves people asking Him difficult questions or for His opinion, which He is always ready to give. If He named the club He couldn't very well refuse to let me join.

We were all really excited when the bell rang.

Beeyatreechee yelled, "Oh, I forgot. Daddy says we have to do one good thing a month, like visiting the old or saving our money to buy something for the poor and needy and helping with the housework for somebody sick, or collecting papers and bottles and selling for worthy projects and things like that."

That night at dinner I told Him about it, emphasizing our program of good works. He was very attentive and leaned over and asked me many questions. When I was through Fatso sneered and said she thought it was a real kids' idea.

He said, "Marian, in contrast to my usual advise to you, will you kindly fill your mouth with something?"

When I told Him we would be getting jackets my heart sank. He hates spending money. I don't know if we are poor but to hear Him go on you would think we were on our way to the poorhouse. He even goes through the garbage to see what is thrown out. Last week He got after Her because the potato peelings were too thick.

"You are throwing away half the potato, half the potato! It's sheer waste! Sheer waste! Don't you know most of the world is starving? What goes into the garbage can around here would feed the population of Bangladesh!"

Well, anyway, to get back to the club, I said Dr. Schinbein

thought He was a walking encyclopedia and we all wanted him to choose the name.

It worked! He beamed. I mean it. He really beamed!

"I'll look into it immediately," He said. He gulped down his tea and scurried up to his Bluebeard's castle.

Today my Latin teacher, Mr. Cooper-Smythe, asked me to stay after class. He has a rather forbidding character and I was not looking forward to it. He is very, very tall, maybe six and a half feet, and he has a steel plate in his head from the war. His hearing is also affected and he has this habit of putting his hand behind his ear and shouting, "Eh? What's that? Speak up! Eh?"

I stood there in front of his desk and he said, "Oh, yes, Isabel McMurry," as if he was expecting somebody else. Then he said, "Your Latin leaves a great deal to be desired. If you continue on your present course you are headed for a D. Or possibly even an E. We don't go any lower than that or who knows to what depths you might plummet."

I didn't say anything.

He said, "Are you listening? Eh?"

"Yes, sir," I said.

"Isabel, do you try to be deliberately obtuse?"

"No, sir," I said.

"Do you know what obtuse means?" he asked.

"No, sir," I said.

"I can't understand it," he said. "I simply cannot understand it. Miss Swanson tells me at our staff meetings that you show unusual promise. If you can do it in *her* English class, why not in *my* Latin class? Eh?"

Before I could tell him that I *can* speak English and I *can't* speak Latin, he said,

60

"Well, I don't know where they got you from. Marian is my best pupil and Bud, I mean Charles, was brilliant, absolutely brilliant."

"I'm adopted," I said.

"Eh?" he shouted, with his hand behind his ear. "What did you say?"

"I said I'm adopted," I shouted back politely.

"Don't be ridiculous," he shouted back again. "Your resemblance to Charles is uncanny, quite uncanny. Even before hearing your name, when you walked into my Latin class, I knew who you were."

I stood there trying to look downcast.

"It's a four-year course. Since you find the first so difficult, perhaps you'll drop it?"

He sounded sort of hopeful.

"No, sir. My father says I have to take it and if you taught Greek here I'd have to take that, too."

"Eh?" he shouted. "What's this about Greek? We are discussing your Latin marks. Don't be insolent!"

So I shouted at the top of my voice what my father had said again and he said, "Fortunately, although I am qualified to teach Greek, because of this school's curriculum, we are both spared that possibility."

I just stood there not knowing if he was through or not.

Finally he said, "Well, I suppose it was too much to ask for three in a row. Very well, Isabel, apply yourself to the best of your ability. You might ask Marian to look over your homework with you, or perhaps your father might consider a tutor. It couldn't do any harm, and who knows? God willing, it might possibly even help."

I knew He would see my report card anyhow, so I brought the subject up at the dinner table, sparing myself nothing.

He rubbed his chin and said, "A tutor? A tutor? Marian? Marian?"

Why do grownups always repeat themselves? If I went around saying "About my Latin, about my Latin, about my Latin," He'd say for God's sake child, get the marbles out of your mouth and come to the point.

He said, "Marian. Hmmm. Marian. What do you think of that?"

Well, to make a long story short, she loves giving advice so she said maybe, if she wasn't too busy. Then she went on to say that Mr. Cooper-Smythe is a prominent classical scholar and loves Latin, but only likes teaching to good pupils. She says if you don't show promise he just can't be bothered.

He sat looking at us as if wondering where we came from, a sort of surprised look, his elbows on the table and his chin resting on his palms. He said,

"If she passes, there will be a healthy bonus for you, Marian."

"How much?" asked Marian, who is no fool.

"Don't be so mercenary," He said. "She's your sister, not mine."

"Yeah?" shouted Marian, "how come she always gets special treatment?"

"I don't!" I shouted

"I don't get any special tutoring and you do so! And you're always playing up to Daddy to get what you want!"

"Of all the big rotten lies!" I shouted. "You're the one who's always playing up!"

"Oh, shut up, both of you!" He shouted and then repeated that crack about having made of his realm a second Africa, fertile only in monsters.

Marian and I both scowled at Him so He kind of backed off and said, "The offer of money will be a fair one, Marian. I imagine you'll earn it.

"It will teach you the value of money," He says. "If you are going to fritter it away on useless things, then you may as well start contributing to your board around here instead."

He says there's nothing like a few little deterrents in life to keep people on their toes, and that after the upbringing *his* children get they will be able to stand on their own two feet and know a fact when they see one.

Last night I dined with the Colonel. He has been saying he was going to ask me for two years and lo and behold, he finally got around to it. My father was very curious and said, "He didn't ask me to dine, too, did he?"

I explained that no, it was just me. I couldn't go into all the explanations about Carruthers and Rommel, etc.

My father said, well see that you're clean and neat then. I wore my best dress, which is unbelievably hideous, but is the only thing that is what Marian calls formal. Wouldn't you know it, it's a lousy baby pink, and was handmade for Marian when she was eleven by Aunt Ada. Marian has always been bigger than me at the same age, if you follow me. (Actually, Marian isn't really fat; she's five foot six and weighs about a hundred and thirty.) This rotten pink dress is kind of short for me. It has hand-smocking across the front which Marian said is very valuable and she is going to put it away and keep it when I am through with it. I'm through with it right now.

Marian said I couldn't possibly go to a "formal" dinner in jeans or a skirt and sweater. Marian also fixed my hair for me. My hair is my best feature, as it is long and thick and naturally curly. Oh, how I wish I were blonde like beautiful Jane Lonsdale. Her hair is the color of cream. When I was about five my hair was so fair it was almost white. By the time I was nine it was sort of dark gold and now it's a gorgeous mud color. I should be grateful it's thick and curly. Marian brushed it all back and tied it with a pink ribbon. It looked stupid but the dress is so awful that it really didn't make much difference.

When I got to the Colonel's I was glad I did put on something special because he was all dressed up, too. He wore a short red kind of bolero jacket, a wide cloth belt around his waist, a starched white shirt, black trousers with a satin stripe down the side, and would you believe it, patent-leather slippers with little bows on them. He also had about a thousand medals pinned on his jacket, only he says they are not called medals, but gongs.

We started out by having Bristol Cream in his living room, which he calls the drawing room. Now you might think this is some sort of milkshake, but it's actually a very delicious sherry wine. After seating me he had to get Rommel settled on guard duty on the door from the kitchen into the dining room. The door from the dining room into the living room he barricaded with chairs, just in case Carruthers tried anything funny.

The table looked awfully gorgeous. In the center was a big silver thing about three feet high with little containers attached all around it for flowers, which the Colonel had filled with some of his best from his garden. The silver knives and forks and spoons were as heavy as lead and were all stamped with some kind of crest. Marian had said for heaven's sake don't eat the way you do at home and of course He said what do you mean the way she eats at home, she never eats at home.

Well, anyway, we started out with Campbell's cream-of-mushroom soup. Then we had canned corned beef, fried. (It's called Bully, the Colonel said, and it is his favorite dish.) With it we had boiled new potatoes with chopped parsley, fresh peas with mint from the Colonel's garden, a salad also ditto, and the Colonel made the dressing at the table from a very beautiful cut-glass set of bottles set in a little whirling stand. We have one at home but I can't remember what it's called because we never use it. The Colonel keeps his on the sideboard when it's not in use. With the salad and corned beef we had a bottle of Mouton Cadet, which is another wine.

For dessert we had chocolate ice cream, which is my favorite. Then we had something I've never had before. It's called a savory, and it is thin strips of toast with lots of melted butter on top, topped with anchovies, which are little salty fish. It was simply delicious.

I told the Colonel it was the best dinner I had ever had and that he was a superb cook. He said a good soldier must be capable of doing everything for himself.

We then had coffee and port, another kind of wine, and the Colonel smoked a cigarillo and we never even mentioned Carruthers. We talked about the battle of Leningrad. The Colonel loves war so much and was awfully sorry to have missed the fighting there, but unfortunately the British did not participate in it.

The Colonel told me all about the battle, how Leningrad was besieged for several years and several million people starved to death there.

I gather it was much worse than Bangladesh. I said I didn't think I'd like to be in a war and see all those things but the Colonel said,

"Nonsense, McMurry."

(He always calls me McMurry.)

"Nonsense, you know nothing about it at all, McMurry. If you had been in only one battle, you would know it is the most supreme moment of life! Nothing can compare to it. The exhilaration when one is as fearless as the gods! The exultation when one's spirit soars in the tumult of battle!"

He went on and on about how it called forth the noblest in man, raised him from the ranks of animals to ascend and wield the sword with angels and a lot of other things that I didn't and probably never will understand.

He said, too, "Quite frankly, my dear McMurry, the only one of those Americans I ever cared for was that fellow called Patton. Americans think war is something serious and soldiering is a game. The fact is, McMurry, it's the other way around. Patton knew."

I said I watched *The War Years* documentaries on TV and it made me absolutely sick seeing those poor horses lying around dead in the streets with their legs up in the air and their stomachs swollen and the poor people pushing old baby buggies and carts piled up with their old belongings.

The Colonel said civilians always had and always will suffer during wars and since wars are inevitable one simply didn't think about them if one wanted to win. He said that personally it had never bothered him one whit.

I was shocked. I think that's an awful thing to say but I didn't say so. I should have said something but after him doing all that cooking to entertain me it seemed rude.

No. That's not the real reason. The real reason is that I'm a coward and afraid to contradict him. I looked coward up in the dictionary, and the only word that describes me is craven.

Well, there was no point going on with the discussion so I just sat there being me. Isabel McCraven.

But I know I'm right and he's wrong and nothing will make me change my mind, even if I am too craven to say so.

When I got home Marian and He were waiting with bated breath to hear all about it. He didn't seem very interested in what we had to eat but He was very interested in the war talk.

When I told him what the Colonel said about civilians He said, "Yes, dreadful, isn't it? But that's what makes outstanding generals, and outstanding generals win wars. What a remarkable man."

Marian said she thought the Colonel was an old creep.

Then, for the umpteenth time He said, sort of like a kid, "You don't suppose he'd meet me some time, do you?"

Remembering Rommel posted at the dining room door I said I doubted it but I'd ask again.

Apart from the war talk it was the most super dinner I've ever had.

This evening after we did the dishes, without even a little fight, Fatso helped me with my Latin again. Part of my trouble is that if I don't understand I'm afraid to ask questions, and if Mr. Cooper-Smythe says do you understand I say yes, even though he might be speaking Chinese for all I know. Marian is actually quite smart and explained a lot of points I was not too clear on. We were seated at the dining-room table with our books in front of us and She was washing the kitchen ceiling when He came downstairs with a list in his hand.

"Here are some suggestions for your club name. I myself rather fancy this one—'Camorra.' It has a pretty sound, yet sinister. It was an early, outlawed, underground Italian movement, like the Mafia, except it was based in Naples, not Sicily."

I went over the list and the name did seem to fit. I thanked him and said I'd take the list to our first meeting, which is to be some time this week.

Well, you'll never guess where the first meeting was held.

Here!

You could have knocked me over with a feather when He suggested it. I was worried about Her. I mean, the last time I brought some kids home She was out scrubbing the driveway on her hands and knees.

He must have read my mind because He said, "Don't worry about Mother. I'll give her one of her pills early and see she's in bed."

I must have looked relieved because He said, "You girls don't ever have to be ashamed of your mother. She's the finest woman alive. There is nothing the matter with her, really. She is merely taking a short vacation, which is the only sane thing to do when you are faced with an overwhelming situation."

There are times when my father quite amazes me.

Then He asked if it was customary to serve refreshments. I said I didn't know but Marian said of course it was. She said she could bake a couple of squares from a mix and ice them if I would make the sandwiches.

What with everybody being so nice and helpful to me at the same time, I was speechless.

You never have to worry about our house being clean because Mumma spends about fourteen hours a day scrubbing it in case Bud should come home early.

They were to come at eight so we had an early dinner, which I couldn't eat because I was so excited. By seven all the good china and silver was set out and the sandwiches were in the fridge.

At eight I seated the girls in the living room. I felt like the Queen entertaining at Buckingham Palace.

About two minutes later he came in and said,

"Good evening, ladies. How charming you all look tonight. An auspicious start for a new venture."

Out in the kitchen I whispered to Fatso what's the matter with him, how come he's so nice to them?

She gave me her oh, you're stupid look.

"Because He likes women, dummy. Haven't you noticed?"

I sure hadn't. "But," I said, "they're not women. They're all thirteen except Beeyatreechee and she just turned fourteen."

"Can you count? In five year's time how old will Beeyatreechee be?"

"Nineteen," I said.

"Exactly. My friends are younger than nineteen but I usually try to bring only the homely ones home. He doesn't like homely women."

"*Him?*" I said. I was genuinely aghast.

"Yes, Him. Get out the lump sugar and the tongs. Do I always have to think of everything?"

"Gee!" I said. "Do you mean Daddy's a bono Fido dirty old man, like Professor Halden?"

"Naaaaw!" Marian said. "You're too young to understand. Honestly, I get so tired of having to explain everything to you. What I'm trying to say is that he never really grew up. He likes flirting with girls because it makes him feel young. Like he was sixteen again. Now do you understand?"

"No," I said.

"I didn't think you would. Listen, it's like this. He left home when he was just a kid and he didn't have time to flirt. He was too busy making a living and getting ahead. And then he married Mumma, see? So he never flirted and now he's making up for lost time. Get it?"

"I guess so."

"Actually, when you think about it, it's kind of sad, you know."

I thought about it and Marian is right. It is sad.

I'm going to have to start flirting. I sure don't want to end up like him.

The trouble is, how do you start? And on whom? I would die of embarrassment trying to flirt with Conn O'Rourke, which is very odd because he's the only one I would want to flirt with.

Well, He went back to his den and the meeting began. We voted for the names on the list and sure enough, Camorra was chosen.

Then Naomi said instead of having the name of our club printed in big vulgar letters on the backs of our jackets, why didn't we have little felt daggers appliquéd to our right hip pockets and Camorra printed on that, like real eighteenth-century Italians. She said her uncle could probably get it done for us cheap. We all agreed on that.

Then we voted for president. Beeyatreechee won hands-down because the club had been her idea. It was a secret ballot and when we voted for secretary I voted for me.

I never thought I would get it, of course, but I thought it would be nice to have one vote even if it were only my own. Imagine my surprise and joy when I was elected with seven out of ten votes!

Oh, I'm so happy I can't sleep. I finally belong to something like other people. I'll be the best secretary the Camorras will ever have. I keep looking up at the real Anne and wishing she were here to share my joy. The tea and sandwiches and squares, everybody said, were delicious, and Mumma's good china and silver and all the old antiques looked elegant. We don't have stereo or records like other people, but everybody laughed and talked until eleven. It was the very best evening of my entire life.

Fatso came home absolutely livid. He was having tea in the kitchen with Mumma and Fatso threw her schoolbooks on the floor and said, "This is the end! The absolute living end!"

I was making cinnamon toast at the counter. He said, "What's the matter and pick up your books. If there's one thing I can't stand it's seeing books abused."

Fatso pointed her finger at me and yelled, "It's her! It's her!"

"I don't wish to be pedantic, but it is she," He said.

"She's absolutely impossible! And after me helping with her club and everything! I have never been so humiliated in my life!'

"Calm down," He said, "and start at the beginning."

"You bet I will!" she shouted. "That—that idiot there—she told everybody at school we had a gardener and that bitchy Beeyatreechee told everybody in the whole school that we haven't got a gardener at all, that we've just got some old rubby-dub who mows the lawn twice a month because you're too lazy to do it! Now everybody in class is asking how my gardener, my cook, my nanny, my maid, and my footman are! I have never, never been so humiliated." She pointed her finger at me again.

"You are a rotten little creep!"

"Beeyatreechee sounds like a singularly unpleasant little girl," He said. "Isabel, you really must stop exaggerating."

Then he gave his tee-hee snicker and said, "Why don't you tell your friends it's really your old rubby-dub dad out there mowing the lawn?"

Marian stamped her foot. "It's not fair! It's not fair! I get hell for being a few minutes late on a date and you let her get away with murder!"

A gross canard, as He would say, if ever I heard one.

She ran out and slammed the kitchen door.

When I went to sit down He pulled my chair out carefully and seated me, then He folded the tea towel over his arm and said, "Will there be anything else, Madam?"

You just never know with him. I laughed. I really couldn't help it, although it was rotten of Beeyatreechee to do that. But poor old Fatso is always, always so—how do you say it? Always so right about everything. Maybe I shouldn't belly-ache about that. Somebody around here has to be right about something sometime and she was good about getting me into the Camorras.

Yesterday, pursuant (new word) to having absolutely nothing to do and no money to spend, I went over to the Colonel's.

His flowers are very gorgeous now and he's getting very close to his black rose, he says. It's in a special greenhouse with the glass painted white and he won't even let me see it.

The black rose is going to be called Lady Clementine, he says, after Sir Winston Churchill's wife.

"Come, we shall play in the billiard room," he said. At the top of the stairs, going down to the billiard room, is a gold-framed portrait of a woman wearing ostrich feathers in her hair. I had often wondered who it was.

The Colonel saw me staring at it.

"My wife. The late Lady Edwina," he said. "Disgusting teeth. Dead for years. Don't dawdle. Everything is set up."

It was cool in the billiard room. I like it down there. It has all sorts of guns and knives and spears on the walls. One spear is from the Mahdi's army when they killed General Chinese Gordon at Khartoum. I saw Charlton Heston on TV in the movie so I know all about it. And there's a cavalry saber that the Colonel's great-great-great grandfather, Lord Raglan, carried at the Charge of the Light Brigade.

There is a bar in the billiard room.

"Care for a drink?" the Colonel asked. "The sun isn't over the yardarm but in this heat we may be excused."

I had a ginger beer and he had a brandy and soda, and he told me more about the war. We had a good game. I've learned a lot. At first he paid me a dollar a game but I enjoy it so much I felt guilty taking it so I told him I'd do it for nothing.

He said, "McMurry, you're a gentleman." Then he looked over his shoulder and whispered, with his white, waxed mustache tips trembling, "Not like Carruthers!"

We are safe from Carruthers in the billiard room. "Switzerland," he calls it. Neutral territory. He gave me two pegs, which is English for a drink. I am learning to speak real English.

Fatso came home furious and close to tears again today because she came third in school, beat by the Chinese twins, Lily and Toy Wong. She was always first in the whole school until Toy and Lily moved here.

It's rather confusing to explain because I really don't understand all of it myself. You see, Canada's immigration policy has been letting in billions of East Indians, Pakistanis, Sikhs, and Chinese.

In our school we have a lot of what are called Hong Kong Chinese. They are very rich, and for some reason unbeknownst to me, very smart.

The white kids mostly hate them. They call the Chinese "slopes" and the East Indians "rag-heads" and the current joke is "Keep Canada green. Paint a Paki."

My father is very much against these sorts of remarks and is always giving us lectures.

"Now, Maid Marian," He said to her when she was raging about the Wong twins, "we were all immigrants once. Mum's parents, my parents."

"We're different," shouted Marian. "They come in here with their money and take all the business over and force up the price of real estate, or else they eat nothing but rice and live a hundred to a house and they haven't done anything to build this country and they're taking jobs away from us and I hate them! That Hong Kong family, the Chews, just bought up the old Woodward estate for five hundred thousand dollars. Five hundred thousand dollars cash! And Rhea's father says they're going to subdivide it up for town houses and make three million from it!"

"Well, well," He says, smiling, "I didn't know we had a Communist in the family."

"Oh, Daddy!" She was shrieking now. "You know what I mean! And with the rate of unemployment, why, why, do they let them in when *we* can't get jobs?"

I said, "The rag-heads in the east end are getting beat up every day by the white kids."

"Oh, shut up!" she shouted. "What's that got to do with the issue, stupid!"

He turned to me. "Don't use that term."

"Well," I said, "you let her call me stupid. And in case you don't know it, and call them what you like, they're moving into West Vancouver. I saw one working at Weller's Garage yesterday. He doesn't speak English and he wears a turban. He's about sixteen, I think. He doesn't have a long beard yet."

"Ah, yes," He said. "A turban. Then he is probably a Sikh. A noble race. Warrior caste. They don't cut their hair and must always wear an iron bracelet and a knife. Splendid looking people. I traveled briefly through India once. Ah, the Rajput, the magnificent carriage of the men. And the women! Not veiled like your meek Moslem women, but bold-eyed as panthers and as beautiful as hoories."

At least, that's what the last word sounded like.

Fatso left the table whining and grumbling and He winked at me and said my poor sister had a lot to learn in this life.

Wow! Wait till I tell you what happened yesterday!

I was walking along the beach at Ambleside, not Dundarave, and feeling very sort of lonely. Anyhow, there was this guy lying on the sand and he sat up when he saw me and said "Hi," so I said "Hi." He said it was a nice day for a walk and I said yes. He said it was kind of lonely and would I like to sit down, so I did. He said his name was Rod and he was twenty-two. I said my name was Ann and I was seventeen.

He asked about what school I went to and stuff like that. When I asked what he did he said he was a divinity student, whatever that is. Well, we talked about movie stars and pop singers for a while and one thing led to another and he said,

"Say, how about us going to McDonald's?"

Well, you could have knocked me over with a feather. I mean, twenty-two and all that.

He said, "I'll bet you'd like a Big Mac and a chocolate shake and fries and maybe a cherry turnover." I said I certainly would be delighted and so we went to his car.

We had only driven about three blocks and I had been looking out the window as I was talking. When I turned to look at him, well, you wouldn't guess in a million years!

He had his *THING* out! Well, you could really have knocked me over with a feather. For a minute I was so stunned I didn't know what to do. Then I said, "Please let me out at the next corner."

He didn't say anything, but he stopped at the next corner and I got out.

I was really mad. We never eat out and I never get to go to McDonald's.

I walked all the way home because all I had was a dime. I was dying to tell someone so I phoned Bonnie on the way home and asked her to meet me the next day after school as it was important.

Bonnie was waiting in her car under the chestnut tree and I jumped in and told her everything.

I thought she would feel sorry for me and put her arm around me and say, "Gee, you poor kid," but she sure as hell didn't. She got *mad*!

She said, "Isabel! For God's sake! Didn't your mother ever tell you not to take rides with strange men?"

Then she sort of quieted down and said,

"Oh, no, of course she didn't." Then she got mad again and shook me real hard and said,

76

"Don't you *ever* do that again, do you hear me? I thought you had more sense than that!"

I turned my face away because I thought I was going to cry and she said, "You look at me and promise me never, never, to do that again." So I did.

"All right. Now don't cry. You know I'm not just trying to be mean. It's for your own sake."

Then she said, "Did you get his license number?"

"What for?" I said. "I don't want to see him again."

"For the police, you silly goose!"

Well, I nearly jumped out the car window!

"You're not going to tell the police?" I said, absolutely aghast.

"I most certainly am!" she said. "Do you want some other little girl raped or murdered?"

"He didn't rape or murder me, all he did was take out his—"

But she cut me short and shouted, "I *know* what he did!"

She said she wouldn't give the police my name, so I needn't worry about that, but I had to give her a description of the car and him.

"You promise not to give my name?"

"Of course!" So I did.

She said, "Go on, think harder. Did he have any unusual physical characteristics or marks?" I said the tip of his little finger was missing but I couldn't remember which hand, and she said good, very good, if he had a record they would have no trouble finding him.

Then she said, "The pig! The dirty pig! When a little girl can't even walk on the damn beach. He's going to be the sorriest son-of-a-bitch in West Vancouver. And why, I ask you, just why aren't the police patrolling that beach to protect people from perverts like that, I would like to know?"

West Van's supposed to have one of the best police forces in the world. They are mostly ex-Mounties. Well, I don't envy them by the time Bonnie's through with them.

Miss Swanson announced something very exciting to the class yesterday. There is going to be a literary competition and there will be a prize for it.

We are all to write a short story, any kind we want, or an essay, or a personal experience.

I was delighted. I went right home and wrote a beautiful and sad tale about a lovely girl who is dying in a hospital. The only window in the room looks out on a blank wall, so every day until she dies she imagines a different scene. One is a gorgeous garden, and she goes over each flower bed in her imagination, planting her favorite flowers and trying to remember the scent of lavender, roses, carnations, and other flowers.

Another time she is on the seashore at sunset and she watches the colors reflecting on the waves and the smell of salt water and seaweed and the roar as the waves crash down and the sucking sound as they draw back.

Then she is a little girl at her first day at school and she has on a new starched dress and her mother has given her twenty-five cents for being brave and she remembers the smell of the newly varnished floors and desks.

She thinks about the scents so much because the hospital smells of ether and Listerine and disinfectant.

Then, at the end of the story, she hears the sound of a hammer hitting nails. She looks out her window, which is in a castle now, and there is a prince building a ladder. He puts it against the castle and climbs up. He is as magnificently dressed as she is. She wears a gown of white brocade with a bodice just under her armpits, and long, long sleeves that hang to the ground. Her gown is embroidered with silken peacocks and sprigs of roses and her hair is hidden with a long stiff pointed cap with a veil hanging down the back. Around the bottom of the cap are emeralds set in a band of gold. He wears skintight green pants, turned-up shoes, a short grey silk jacket with puff sleeves with slashes that show tufts of scarlet velvet. On his head he wears a little round scarlet velvet cap with pearls all over it and at the side of it is stuck an ostrich plume. One of my old fairy books had a colored picture just like that with her sitting before him on a horse.

When he gets to her room he takes her in his arms and carries her to the ladder and they escape. Actually, this is when she dies.

Two years ago when I was in the hospital having my tonsils out my throat began to bleed inside and it wouldn't stop. They put me in a room with two other girls and I had blood transfusions.

One of the girls was an Indian from away up past the Chilcotin, really far away. She could understand English but she didn't speak much. Maybe she didn't want to. She hardly ever talked.

The other girl's mother was in Acapulco having a nervous breakdown because this girl had leukemia, like the Indian girl. Nobody ever visited either of them. They were both fifteen.

After a few days, the bleeding in my throat stopped, but they wouldn't let me go home.

The girls just lay there with their faces turned sideways. The white girl had been taking drug treatments and all her hair had fallen out and she wore a red wig.

"Why red?" I asked her.

She said she always wanted to have red hair.

My father only visited me once. He was as white as a sheet and shaking all over. He only stayed a few minutes. He left a big box of chocolates and practically ran out of the room. Marian told me after that he told her he has a horror of hospitals and sick people and death. He thought I was going to die, I guess, which is kind of dumb because it never even occurred to me. Maybe he remembered his little sisters.

The nurses wouldn't let me eat the chocolates and the two girls didn't want any. They hardly ate anything. Marian came one afternoon so I gave her the chocolates. They were all gone by the time I got home.

The white girl was the one who told me they both had leukemia. The hospital has a marvelous view of the harbor but the girls never looked at it. They didn't read, either, or watch the little TV set the white girl's mother had bought for her.

Sometimes the white girl would do fancy work on an embroidery hoop for a few minutes, then she would sigh and lay it down and turn her face aside. I asked her if she felt sick and was in pain and she just smiled and nodded.

So I got out of bed and walked down the hall. A nurse stopped me and nearly had a fit. They had just taken that blood thing out of my arm. She said I was to get right back in bed.

I asked why somebody didn't give the two girls with leukemia something to make them feel better.

She looked at me very crossly and asked who said they had leukemia. I was afraid I would get them into trouble if I told so I said I just guessed and she said, "Well, then you have guessed wrongly. They are here for tests and nothing else. Now young lady, get back in that bed and stay there!"

I felt so sorry for them that I began to tell them stories even though I wasn't supposed to talk because of my throat. I wasn't even sure if they listened.

In the middle of the night I would hear the Indian girl crying. She never did in the daytime. I guess she was homesick and missed her people.

This time it was in the middle of the night when I was telling them a story. It was all about the beautiful things they would see if they looked out the window and I couldn't think of an ending so I just stopped. I was suddenly very tired and I didn't know if they were both listening anyway. After a minute they both whispered at the same time, "Please go on."

So I finished the story of the princess, only I didn't say she died.

When I left, the white girl gave me her embroidery. I never finished it; it wouldn't have been hers if I did. It's in tissue paper in the desk drawer with some of my many other valuables which I will list later, if anybody is interested.

It took a week for all the stories to be written and another week to judge them. Everybody was wondering who would win and what the prize would be.

Beeyatreechee said it would be a book because that's what they always are and she bet she would win it and did anyone want to bet with her and nobody did. She had written a Biblical story about how Ruth had felt as she stood amid the alien corn. I'll bet her father wrote it for her. That's what her story was called: "Amid The Alien Corn." I had to admit it was a good title. It was better than either of mine. My first title was "The Window of Sorrow and Joy," but later I changed that and called it "The Two-Way Window."

Anyhow, to make a long story short, the day finally came, and guess who won!

Me!

Miss Swanson called me up to the front of the class.

Beeyatreechee was right about one thing. The prize was a book—Palgrave's *Golden Treasury of Verse*, bound in red leather with gold letters on the cover.

Miss Swanson said never had she read such a touching story by one so young, and she read it to the class. One girl actually cried when she heard it (me).

Then she presented the book and said she predicted a great future for me.

Even He, as we sat at Bangladesh that evening, was impressed and said, "Well, well, so we have a Brontë in the family. Which are you: Emily, Charlotte, or Anne?"

I said I was Anne, because that's my favorite name. Then old Fatso said she bet I was Branwell. I didn't get it. He laughed and said,

"Marian, that is a cruel remark. I think you should apologize to your sister and congratulate her."

She did. She did it to get on the right side of him.

Then He said, "I am very proud of you, Isabel," and then He went and spoiled *that* by saying, "I hope you will try to do as well in your other subjects."

Minnesota gets straight A's in everything. Natch.

Later I looked up the Brontë sisters in the encyclopedia and found out that Branwell was their nutty brother.

Last night Marian and Rhea Schinbein went to Jane Lonsdale's home. I was sort of hoping maybe Jane would invite me along, but she didn't. I guess maybe she thinks I'm kind of young, even though she did want me for a little sister. That's my trouble. I look awfully young and people always think I am immature mentally as well.

I asked Marian if Jane was still going to marry Fraser Shinbein and Marian just shrugged. Then I asked *why* would Jane want to marry him and Marian said it was a complete mystery to her.

Dr. Shinbein is in real estate as well as being a doctor. He owns a waterfront apartment building in West Vancouver and is very rich. As a matter of fact, Marian says if you own a waterfront apartment building in West Vancouver you are not only very rich, but very, very rich.

Maybe Jane was marrying Fraser for his money? Marian says no, Jane would never do a thing like that. She doesn't care about money and is going to start training as a registered nurse as soon as the next course opens in a couple of months. After she graduates she intends to do children's nursing in Africa.

Where Fraser is going to be when this mercy work is going on, Marian says, she doesn't know. Maybe he'll just sit under a palm tree sniffing cocaine.

Maybe Jane really loves him, I said, and Marian made a face and said *yuhkkk* or however you spell it.

I said that the whole thing didn't make sense and she said well, if you're so smart, tell me. Then she said Jane's parents really are as dull as Jane said they were. She thought maybe Jane was exaggerating but that our home is fascinating compared to theirs and she would go to Timbuktu if she had to live with the Lonsdales.

Sometimes I go for ages and don't write in my diary, which is very bad as He says discipline is the most important qualification a writer can have.

He should know. He's had a lot of very dull books published.

Some days I don't even look up my word. Today I did and my word is purvey: to cater, provision, or furnish. Try working that into the conversation.

Wanted, purveyed room to share.

Jane Lonsdale is marrying Fraser Schinbein and they are having a big purveyed wedding.

I am leaving on Tuesday for a weekend hike up Mount Everest. My equipment includes a tent, twenty Sherpas, a down sleeping bag, and twenty pounds of dried purveys.

Everybody is crazy except me.

Well, He came in purple in the face this afternoon, panting like Peggy, and clenching and unclenching his fists. I know better than to say anything when He is like this so I just hid behind the book I was reading.

But not Marian.

"What's the matter, Daddy?" asked old Dumbo.

"I just walked all the way up that goddamn hill, that's what's the goddamn matter!" He shouted.

"Why didn't you drive?" asked Stupido.

He took his shoes off in the middle of the stairs and threw them at the front door.

"I did not drive because the goddamn car did not work and the reason that the goddamn car did not work was that down at the goddamn gas station Gunga Dean put water in my goddamn gas tank and that's why I did not drive!"

The hill from the gas station up to our place is really very steep and long.

When He got upstairs I heard him ranting, "Jesus Christ! Why is the whole of humanity conspiring to drive me stark raving mad?"

Mumma came in with the tea and cookies. She put them down and stroked my hair.

Fatso scowled and started gobbling chocolate-chip cookies.

"Who was Gunga Dean?" I asked Fatso.

"Oh, look it up in the encyclopedia!" When he gets mad at her, she gets mad at me. I'm used to it.

So I did look it up and it wasn't Gunga Dean but Gunga Din and it was a poem written by Rudyard Kipling.

I started to laugh. I really couldn't help it. Gunga Din was a Hindu. Probably a Paki. I laughed and laughed and finally Marian said what's so funny.

"You won't believe this," I finally managed to gasp, "but Gunga Din was a water carrier."

At dinner that night He looked at me and said, "I do not want to hear one word, not one word, do you understand, from you."

"What did I do?" I said.

He said, "Young lady, if you are looking for a thick ear, I don't know of a quicker way of getting one."

I don't know what a thick ear is, but if He is handing them out I don't want any.

We no longer discuss Canada's immigration policy at the table.

Tonight we talked about what English would be like if there had been no Norman Conquest. He and Marian had lots of fun trying to speak in sentences using only words with Anglo-Saxon roots.

I'm only sure of one and I don't think they would like to hear it at the dinner table.

After dinner Fatso told me what really killed him. As he was huffing and puffing up the hill, Mr. Wong, in his Silver Cloud Rolls-Royce, drove right past him.

What is the matter with me? Why do I look like I'm about ten years old instead of like other girls my age? They all have got their periods, but not me.

I asked Bonnie the last time I saw her. I didn't know quite how to put it and hemmed and hawed until finally she lost patience with me and said, "Oh, for goodness sakes, Isabel, if you have something to say, say it."

I said that I wasn't developing along normal lines. She sat staring out the car window for a minute and then she said, "Oh."

She looked out the window some more until I began to really worry. Oh, God! I know! I've probably got cancer or venereal disease. I just know it!

"I guess it's serious," I said with a deceptive calmness.

Bonnie turned from the window and said "What is?"

"You can tell me," I said. "I can take it."

"Tell you what?" Bonnie asked.

"I'd rather have the truth," I said. "You can tell me the reason I am not menstruating like normal girls. They have marvelous cures for cancer and syphilis now."

This time Bonnie's head snapped away from the window back to me.

"Isabel," she said, "are you out of your cotton-picking mind? Now what in heaven's name would make you think something as absurd as that? You always let your imagination run away. Or are you feeling even sorrier for yourself than usual?"

Bonnie was turning against me, too!

"Honestly Isabel, you are always complaining. You don't know how lucky you are, believe me, living in such a nice house filled with beautiful antiques."

"They aren't *our* antiques," I said. "They're just old stuff He buys at auctions."

"There you go again!" she said. "You should have been born one of nine kids on a farm in northern Saskatchewan like me! Your father may be a nut, but when it comes to mean men, my father beat them all. We spoke when we were spoken to and not before. And the house was just a house, a place to eat and sleep in. Nothing nice or pretty like yours. By the time my mother was forty she looked seventy. The land was everything. Buy more land every year, even if you have to work your own kids into the ground to get it. And guess who will inherit it—the boys, that's who. When my eldest sister got married did she get land for a wedding gift? Not bloody likely, I can tell you. She got a hundred dollars, four homemade goose down pillows and a cow, and that's all she'll ever get. And do you know how much the old man is worth? Well, counting everything it must be over a million in land and equipment, and the boys will get everything.

"I was smart. I ran away to Moose Jaw when I was fifteen. I looked old for my age. I got a job in a restaurant. It was all I could get, waitress work, see, because all I knew was farming and housework. Boy, no matter how tough things get, I only have to remember that farm to count my blessings."

Well, I certainly wouldn't have even brought the subject up

if I knew I was in for a lecture like this. All I did was make a simple inquiry on maturity, that's all.

Now it was my turn to stare out my side of the car window.

Bonnie lit a cigarette and smoked and I continued to look.

"*Now* what's the matter?"

"Nothing," I said. "Nothing at all, thank you." I was very formal.

"Oh, Isabel!" she said. "Stop feeling so sorry for yourself and quit sulking. Really, you are the limit. Sometimes I think you push me just to see how far you can go."

I thought she would add, "Like Bud," but she didn't.

I pretended to yawn and kept looking out the window, but then my chin began to wiggle. If Bonnie doesn't love me, who will?

Bonnie said, "Oh, come on, now, Isabel." And of course then I began to blubber. Bonnie put her arm around me and said, "Oh, come on, don't cry. Now, Isabel, you just quit that. You know perfectly well you haven't got cancer or syphilis. The only thing the matter with you is that you're very young for your age. Underdeveloped. Immature."

I squinched my lips together so I wouldn't cry anymore.

"What I mean is," Bonnie said very quickly and hastily, "physically, not mentally. You'll be grown-up before you know it. Just you wait and see."

I guess she could tell I still felt sort of hurt, because she said, "Dry your tears and cheer up, and if you do I'll tell you a bit of juicy scandal."

"What?" I said.

"Well," she said, "you know Fraser Schinbein? He came into the restaurant where I work about one o'clock the other night and he was absolutely stoned. On drugs as well as booze, I'm positive. He got really nasty with one of the girls and when the manager asked him to leave, he punched the manager. His eyes were glittering and he looked as nutty as a fruitcake. Well, the manager told him to leave and he wouldn't. He said he wanted a meal. The manager told him the kitchen closed at midnight and this guy started using language that I certainly wouldn't want you to hear. The manager finally told this Schinbein guy to either shut up or get out. How old is he, anyway?"

"Twenty-two."

"Well then, he's no kid. He started getting really rough and the manager called the cops. They took him away, but I heard that his father came right down with a lawyer and got him out."

She looked at me expectantly. "Well, how does that strike you? Makes you forget your problems, eh?"

"Yeah," I said. "I guess everyone's got problems."

"Take my word for it, Isabel, I mean Ann, I'd rather have yours than theirs. You mark my words, you'll be a big girl before you know it."

Bonnie is really a wonderful person.

Yesterday the most terrible thing happened when Peggy and I were walking on the beach.

I looked up at the mountains and there was this great big brown scab on them. I couldn't believe my eyes.

I ran back to the Italian workmen. They all known me now.

"What's happened to the mountains?' I cried and pointed. They began to talk all at once in Italian and they laughed.

The foreman, Primo, who speaks the best English said, "You don't look at the mountains a lot. You never saw that before?"

"What is it?" I cried, aghast.

He said it had been like that for weeks. They are building a big ski resort up there. Next winter when the snow is there many people will go skiing up there.

When I got home I was so upset I just sat on the back porch with my arm around Peggy's neck.

At dinner time I told them what had happened to our mountains.

Marian said, "Oh, for goodness sakes, Isabel, it's been a political issue for years, and it was in the paper for months and months, and they started work up there ages ago. If you read anything except Ann Landers you'd know what it was all about. Besides, you're always bellyaching because nothing ever happens and as soon as anything changes you bellyache because it does."

The trouble with her is she's too damn smart. She thinks she knows everything.

I looked at Him but He just shrugged.

"I'm going to save my money and learn to ski," said Fatso.

"It's awful. It's horrible!" I said. "First the beaches and now the mountains. It's rotten."

He shrugged again and said, "You may as well get used to it. Already one generation, born in the era of horse-drawn carriages, has lived to see men walk on the moon. You'd better prepare yourself for a few more cultural shocks in the future if a ski resort upsets you. Never in the history of man has change been so rapid and radical. It's as if man's mind had been programmed by computers a million years ago and the little holes in the brain-card that fulfill scientific development are now being punched."

Words, words, words. What does it all really mean?

Well, He can accept changes if He wants, but I won't. I'll always like the old ways better and I don't care if it is dumb. There are too many people and inventions already.

"Why don't they invent something to feed your old Bangladesh if they're so smart?" I said.

"Search me," he said. "I'm trying to find out, too. Let me know if you come up with anything."

It's a week since I have written in my diary. Yesterday was the blackest day of my life, so far. I don't trust life anymore. I spent the whole night in my room looking up at the real Anne and wishing I was dead like her.

It happened when I came home from school. I should have known because Marian was so nice to me. She goes around with Naomi's older sister, so she already knew. At least, I guess that's how she found out.

The phone rang. Marian answered it and said with a funny look on her face, "It's for you. Sit down."

He and Mumma were in the living room, next to the hall.

It was Debbie Cunningham. She said they had drawn lots for who was to phone me and she lost. She said Martha Koch's family wouldn't let her join the club because they are Jehovah's Witnesses, although I still don't see what that has to do with it.

She said Beeyatreechee told her ten was too many anyhow and nine was uneven so the club ought to have eight members. Then she said she thought I should be the one to go because I was the youngest and a year at that age was like four at any other. Then Beeyatreechee said she didn't want to influence them so they would take a vote.

Debbie said it was a secret ballot but everybody told everybody how they voted anyway, so it wasn't really secret. Debbie said she voted against me because there wasn't any one else to vote against, but three voted for me to stay and if I'd been there and voted for myself I would have won. At least, I think that's what she meant. She sounded sort of mixed up. The only thing I am sure of is that I am not a Camorra any more. Then Debbie said she was sorry and hung up.

I just sat there, the phone in my hand. I tried to imagine the Gestapo coming up the stairs and kicking the door in. It didn't work. I wished I was dead. I wished everything and anything so I wouldn't have to go to school tomorrow.

He said, "Well, Divine Sarah, what's the latest tragedy in your life?"

But Marian said, "Shhhhhhhh!" to him and led him out to the dining room.

I didn't go to the dinner table that night and Mumma brought up a tray as if I were sick, but I couldn't eat.

I couldn't even cry. I just sat and shivered. For the first time the real Anne was no help at all. I guess I must have fallen asleep with my clothes on. When I woke up it was morning.

The strangest thing happened.

Under the door was a white envelope. On it was typed *Nil Desperandum*, which Marian told me later means never despair.

In the envelope was a ten dollar bill. I've never had ten dollars before. I could only think of one person who could have put it there. It sure didn't sound like Marian. I asked her, just in case, but she shook her head and said no.

It must have been Him.

I asked Marian to translate "Surprised but grateful" into Latin for me, then I printed it on a piece of paper, and slid it under his door upstairs.

Neither of us said anything.

School? Well, I needn't have worried. It was as if I had some awful catching disease or I wasn't there. It's funny. They are the ones who hurt me, but they acted as if I had done something wrong and avoided me. I suppose the whole school knows about it and is laughing at me.

I shall remember this until the day I die. I shall never forgive her.

Henceforth her name will be pronounced Beatrice, although I hope I never have to sully my lips by saying it.

He gave me a dollar today. Don't ask me why. He stuck it in my ear, rolled up, as He passed me in the kitchen.

I went down to the Mall. It isn't much fun going by yourself. As a matter of fact it isn't much fun going anywhere by yourself. Except the beach, maybe.

I kept hoping none of the Camorras would see me there by myself.

I bought a hot dog and a milk shake and looked at all the clothing stores. Then I went to the ladies' room.

Somebody had written on the wall, "Marilyn Graham is a fink", so I wrote under it, "So is Beatrice Featherstone."

I wish I could write it in the men's room and that's not what I'd write, either.

I went over to the Colonel's today. It was raining and gray and not much fun. We played canasta and he cheated. So did I. He was in a bad mood because he says winter is coming and he dreads it. I don't understand, because no matter what month of the year it is, winter is always going to come.

He says he doesn't know how he'll get through another one. It's dark and dreary and cold in both the garden and the billiard room and those are the only places he's safe from Carruthers.

To tell you the truth, I'm a little afraid of Carruthers myself, although I have never seen him except for his picture, which the Colonel says I must memorize in case I ever meet him. Carruthers looks young and cool and in command of everything, and his eyes, which are pale, look out over the desert as if he sees something dangerous that he's not afraid of out there. He looks very handsome.

"What is it Carruthers is looking for over the desert?" I asked. "Is it the Germans?"

He shook his head. Once the Colonel told me that there was a mystic bond between the Germans and the Allies in the desert because both were of the same stock and fighting each other in a land that was alien to both of them. It didn't stop them shooting each other, he said, but they were like blood brothers in a terrible, ancient family saga. Saga means a very old story. When I told my Father what the Colonel said He said that the Colonel was a remarkable man.

"What is Carruthers looking for?" said the Colonel in answer to my questions. "Carruthers, like all of us, is looking for death."

That put him off the whole afternoon. The Colonel has a very peculiar disposition. Sometimes he's loads of fun, almost like a boy. He calls me McMurry, and throws cushions, and we have contests to see who can jump over the most chairs or balance a whiskey glass on our foreheads. At other times he's mean right to the bone. I know he's very lonely. I know this because I am lonely. Sometimes I don't know why I play with a mean, lonely old man who cheats at canasta except that I'm a mean young girl who cheats at canasta. I wouldn't with anybody else, and I wouldn't have with him if he hadn't started it. He says it's strategy. Never trust anybody, he says. The point is, he says, that no matter what game you play, your opponent is always your enemy, and whether I like it or not, that's how wars are won. "How do you think I got to be a general?" he said.

A letter from Aunt Ada today. While Fatso and I were sitting in the box room she told me something I didn't know.

Uncle Billy is a Catholic. Marian says it appears he rebecame one to spite Aunt Ada. She, Aunt Ada, that is, spends a great deal of time praying for Uncle Billy, which infuriates him. Marian says he came home with a snootful one night and Aunt Ada went upstairs to her room to pray for him and Uncle Billy carried on like a maniac, just like You Know Who, who, of course, doesn't even drink.

Barney, who can always manage him, calmed Uncle Billy down and explained to Marian that it is because Aunt Ada prays for Uncle Billy in Lutheran that he goes absolutely ape. I said why doesn't Uncle Billy just pray for Aunt Ada in Catholic to even things up but Marian says it doesn't work that way.

Marian once asked Aunt Ada why she doesn't go and see Father O'Shaughnessy, Uncle Billy's parish priest, about Uncle Billy's drinking. Aunt Ada gave a bitter laugh, Marian says, and said "Are you kidding? Father O'Shaughnessy plays poker with your Uncle Billy and drinks him under the table three times a week."

Aunt Ada told Marian that the hardest thing in the whole world for her to do is to pray for Father O'Shaughnessy because he and Uncle Billy talked Barney into becoming a

Catholic. When Barney was nineteen he had to go to church and be baptized, just like a baby. He chose the name Benedict but everybody still calls him Barney. Aunt Ada says his becoming a Catholic is even worse than Dietrich's being a Communist.

I said I thought Communists were against the law, but Marian says they are a perfectly legitimate political party in Canada and you can join them anytime you want as long as you don't mind your mail being steamed open, your telephone tapped, your home searched, and the Mounties breathing down the back of your neck for the rest of your life.

Aunt Ada says she has given up praying for Uncle Billy's soul. Now all that she prays for is that he will develop a conscience, so that when he is roasting in hell at least he will know why. As for Father O'Shaughnessy, Aunt Ada says, he can't hide behind that clerical collar and God will get him.

There are times Aunt Ada is a little harsh in someways. As a matter of fact she sounds more Irish than German.

Aunt Ada says this business about Barney and Dietrich would never have happened if she had not married an Irishman, and if she had had daughters instead of boys.

Today I stayed after school to talk with Miss Swanson. I often do, and she always seems glad to see me. I have a funny feeling she knows about the Camorras, although she didn't mention it. However, she did say, sort out of the blue, "You know, Isabel, my dear, sometimes things happen and you think it's the end of the world, but you know, dear, it is amazing how strong the human spirit is and how it overcomes even seemingly insurmountable difficulties and tragedies. I am not saying one does not still suffer, but one finds the strength to cope."

I just said yes.

Then she changed the subject and started talking about TV and she said she supposed we watched very little in our house.

I didn't know what to say. As a matter of fact we're addicts, all of us.

She said she supposed my father monitored what we viewed and I said yes.

Well, He does, sort of. If He isn't watching it He says keep that damned thing turned down.

Marian is hooked on old movies from 1930 to 1945 and she is an expert on the furniture, clothing, cars, and even speech patterns. She says she nearly fell out of her chair the other night when James Cagney, in a 1931 movie, said "screw" to a guy. And people don't say that they are "sore" anymore when they mean they are angry.

I watched *It Happened One Night* last week, with Claudette Colbert and Clark Gable, which was made in 1934, and I really couldn't figure out why they made such a fuss about hanging that dumb blanket up between them when they shared a room. I watched *Midnight Cowboy* on the late show two weeks ago, and *wow!*

Me, I love travelogues, war documentaries, the old Groucho Marx quiz shows, any animal or zoo features, and all the reruns of the classical pictures. I don't know how often I have seen *Great Expectations,* or *A Christmas Carol,* or *Grand Illusion,* or *The Bridge on the River Kwai* or *Forbidden Games.*

He is a cartoon nut. They bore me silly. I really can't sit through even one. His favorite is Mickey Mouse; He dashes down from his lair, rubbing his hands and shouting, "Okay, kids, let's have a little shot of old Mickey!"

Marian says it's like the toy soldiers and flirting—because he never had a real childhood or youth. She's probably right. She usually is.

I really think I would die of shame if Miss Swanson ever found out that I have a father who thinks Popeye is one of the great characters of the twentieth century.

Marian once said she thought Popeye was awful and vulgar and dumb and what about people like Doctor Albert Schweitzer. He said, oh, that egomaniacal old religious fake, pootling away on his pipe organ among the jungle foliage with one eye on history and the other on the camera.

I looked up pootling in the dictionary but it isn't there.

Marian is mad—boy is she ever. Usually if she gets really mad, He gives in and is especially nice, but this time He is mad, too.

The night before last He went to one of His old antique auctions. Marian asked if she could have a friend in for the evening and He said yes. What she didn't say was it was a boy, a real drip called Jeff Woodward who thinks he is God's gift to women. Anyway, off He went to the auction, but there was nothing He wanted to bid on, so He came home early. He glared and just barely answered when Marian introduced Jeff.

Marian says you'd think she was practicing for a life of prostitution the way He acts about boys. Well, I went off to my room upstairs to read and He went to bed, slamming His door nearly off the hinges.

This twit stayed and stayed and stayed.

Then he started walking around, slamming doors upstairs again. Finally, in a whisper I bet you could have heard on Dundarave Pier, He hissed across the hall from his room to mine,

"Hey, Isabel, what's the matter with that bimbo? Is he some sort of goddamn orphan? Hasn't he got a home?"

Well, of course they heard, but this clod downstairs is so insensitive he just said to Marian, "What's the matter with your old man? Is he stoned or something?"

Marian was put in the awful position of having to suggest it was time he left. I felt sorry for her. I was acutely embarrassed myself and I wasn't even directly concerned.

She wouldn't talk to Him at breakfast and whacked the teapot down in front of him so hard the tea slopped out of the spout. Then she flounced—I believe that is the word—out of the room.

He just snorted and turned to me and said, "Hoity-toity, my lady."

Whatever that is supposed to mean.

Gosh! A big scandal in West Vancouver with everybody whispering and talking at school and even all the grown-ups tsk-tsking.

Fraser Schinbein was arrested by the police on a drug charge. It is very serious as he may be charged with trafficking as well as possession.

Not only is he up on a drug charge, he forged checks in his father's name and even hocked his mother's thirty-thousand-dollar engagement ring when his father wouldn't give him more money. His father refused to press charges.

At school both Rhea and Naomi held their heads very high and acted as though absolutely nothing had happened. Marian says she admires them for it and I guess I do, too.

What about Jane Lonsdale, I asked Marian. Marian says that that is the biggest mystery of all. Jane behaves as if the whole thing is rather boring.

Rhea's parents were furious because they thought Jane and

Fraser were going to get married. Now, Rhea told Marian, they are furious because Jane doesn't seem to care whether Fraser goes to jail or not. Well, obviously, Jane does *not* love him. Why she said she was going to marry him is still a mystery to me.

Another letter from Aunt Ada today; rather a surprise so soon after her last, but no money in it.

We sat on the floor of the box room, and I said shake it again, maybe you missed it. I am broke except for my ten dollars, which I am saving to buy a pair of high-heeled shoes. It will take ages to get enough, but of course, it will be ages before He will let me wear high-heeled shoes. Marian says He seems to think high-heeled shoes are guideposts to the footprints of the Devil.

Anyhow, there wasn't any money and Marian told me not to be so mercenary, which I looked up later and which means, among other things, liking money. I don't know anybody who doesn't.

Aunt Ada said in the letter that the reason she was writing to her girls at this time was that she was buying some very expensive wool to make us Icelandic sweaters for Christmas. Mine she is making two sizes too large so I can grow into it as the wool costs so much it wouldn't be sensible to make it to fit me now when I am growing so much. I don't know why she couldn't wait until I finish growing and in the meanwhile just send me the money.

Since *nothing ever* fits me, I decided not to think about it.

Marian suddenly stopped reading and looked at me oddly.

"Get a load of this," she said, or should I say, sneered. "According to Aunt Ada, we are named after the two little dead sisters."

I was rather touched myself, but Marian said, "Jeez, ain't that enough to melt a heart of stone."

There are times when I think Marian is a great deal like her father.

Oh, I don't know. I just don't know anymore. I haven't written in my diary for ages, and now this. It's worse than the Camorras. I didn't think anything could be, but this is much worse. Is life going to go on being this way? Is this what it's *supposed* to be like?

I was called over the loudspeaker, to the principal's office yesterday morning. My heart was pounding so I could hardly breathe. I didn't know what I could have done. At least, that they'd know about.

Mr. Raymond asked me to sit down.

He didn't beat around the bush. He said, "I'm afraid I have some bad news for you, Isabel. It's about Miss Swanson. I know how fond you have been of her, and she was always talking about you."

What did he mean, she was?

"She's dead. She was killed, Isabel, an hour ago on the Upper Levels Highway, driving here. I didn't want you to hear it from your schoolmates."

I didn't say anything. I just sat there staring at him.

"If you wish to take the rest of the day off I will quite understand."

I never knew he was so nice. I shook my head. I didn't want to go home. Ever. I don't remember one class for the rest of the day.

I wish I could cry but I can't. I never can when I want to and I always do when I don't want to.

Bonnie is the only one I can talk to.

Death is a subject we *never* talk about in this house. They hung him on a meat hook. He lived for three days. I never think about him.

There's a florist shop called Eden's here. I went in with my ten dollars. I ordered a dozen red roses.

When the man saw the ten dollars he shook his head. "It will cost a lot more than that, miss."

I started to go and he said, "Perhaps you'd like to choose something cheaper. A nice plant?"

I shook my head.

"Is it for someone in the hospital?" he asked.

"It's for someone dead."

He said, "Oh, I'm sorry, my dear." Then he said, "Oh, was it Miss Swanson from the school? We've had quite a few orders for her."

I nodded and turned again. I was at the door when he called me back.

"You know, it's the strangest thing. I quite forgot. Someone ordered a dozen red roses and forgot to pick them up. They're perfectly fresh. I think I could let you have them for ten dollars."

I guess maybe there is a God.

Mr. Raymond gave the whole school a half-day off for the funeral.

I didn't go. I phoned Bonnie and asked her to meet me at Dundarave Beach instead of under the chestnut tree.

All the Italians whistled at her when we walked past them. She is very gorgeous. We walked a long way from where they were working and sat on a log. I told her what had happened.

She said, "Oh, honey, I'm sorry. I know how much you loved her and she was always so good and understanding with you."

Then I began to cry.

She said, "Go ahead, get it all out of your system. It's the best thing you can do. I know." She put her arms around me and I really howled. I looked up and she was crying, too.

"Why are you crying, Bonnie?" I said.

"Just to keep you company."

She looked kind of funny, almost gray.

On the way back she stopped the car, got out, and threw up.

"Are you sick, Bonnie?" I said.

"Yeah," she said. "I guess I've got a touch of the flu."

Today I still felt so restless and awful I went over to the Colonel's, but I couldn't even concentrate on dominoes, I felt so rotten. I told the Colonel about Miss Swanson and he said he was sorry, but he really wasn't, he was just saying that. He really doesn't care about anything or anybody except Carruthers. Oh, he's fond of Rommel, pats his head occasionally and calls him a good chap, but nothing except Carruthers goes very deep.

Once I asked him what he would do if Rommel fell asleep during sentry duty, like Napoleon's sentry. Would he shoot Rommel?

The Colonel's bloodshot blue eyes widened with surprise and he said, "Of course. A soldier must do his duty, both I and my sentry. It would be my duty."

It sort of scared me. I like Rommel.

Well, the Colonel wasn't much use about Miss Swanson.

When I was leaving he said, "You must become accustomed to death, McMurry. Life itself is war, and war is death. Stiff upper lip, my dear fellow."

Oh, shit. To hell with everybody.

It's been a long time, again, since I've written in my diary, although I look up my word every day now because I think Miss Swanson would want me to. My word today is obsolete. Obsolete, out-of-date, outworn, disused. All my words seem to have depressing connotations. That's one of the words from last week, connotations.

Well, just to complete my depression, guess who I got for English now. Mr. Cooper-Smythe.

And guess what I got in English. Well, I'll tell you; it was a D.

We had to do a book report and I wrote one on this book called *East Lynne,* which I got out of the classical section of the public library.

It's a super story written over a hundred years ago. It's about this nobleman's daughter, who, incredible as this may sound, is called Lady *Isabel* Vane.

Lady Isabel married a Mr. Carlyle, who is sort of a drip, so she runs away with her seducer, leaving her children with Mr. Carlyle. She is in a railway accident and is left for dead but recovers and, believe it or not, goes to work as a poor governess for her former husband—in disguise, so she can be with her children.

She wears funny clothes and blue glasses, which were quite unusual at that time, and nobody recognizes her, which is sort of stretching a point.

As she sits at the bedside of her little dying boy it is absolutely harrowing. (Another of last week's words. It's always nice to find a really useful use for them.)

Little William, her son, thinks, of course, that she was killed in the railway accident and he wants to join his mother in heaven.

His father, who doesn't know that poor Lady Isabel is sitting at William's bedside that very minute, says only, "My precious boy."

William's sister, Lucy, is brought in—to see him die, I guess—and he says, "Good-bye, Lucy."

"I am not going out," replies Lucy. "We have just come home."

Again William bids her adieu, holding out his cold little hand and again she replies, "Good-bye, William, but indeed I am not going out anywhere."

Down on her knees, her face buried in the counterpane, a corner of it stuffed in her mouth that it might better help stifle her agony, kneels poor Lady Isabel.

Mr. Carlyle thinks she is just the governess and can't understand why she is so upset about William dying. He goes to get his second wife, and William's baby half-sister, and some strawberry juice.

Lady Isabel rises up and flings her arms aloft in a storm of sobs.

"Oh, William darling, let me be to you as your mother."

"Papa has gone for her," says William.

"Not *her*. I—I—," Lady Isabel checked herself and fell, sobbing, on the bed.

No, not even at that last hour when the world was closing on her son dared she say, "I am your mother."

William dies.

I cried buckets.

Mr. Cooper-Smythe called me after class and asked me why I had chosen that particular book.

I said I had found it in the classical section of the library, and did he think there was something the matter with it.

He sighed and said that just possibly, it was the worst book ever written.

I asked Him when I got home and He laughed. Then He stopped laughing and said, "My dear child, you are star-crossed. Why, of all books, did you pick that one?"

He stood looking down at me and then He said, "You know, upstairs in my library are thousands of books. If more than a hundred are used for anything but study, reference, and curiosity a hundred and fifty years from now I shall be very surprised. And yet this dusty little Victorian melodrama touched you to the heart and is still in print. I wish I could write a book that would be read a hundred and fifty years from now, even if it were called *East Lynne*.

"He gave me a D for it," I said.

"Who's to say it's good or no good? You, who enjoyed it, or this pompous pundit Pooper-Smythe? A fig, sir, on your Mr. Pooper-Smythe."

You really never know what to expect from grown-ups. I have a feeling it's going to be just as bad when I'm one of them.

When I was unlocking the Colonel's garden gate this morning, Miss Pettigrew shook her fist at me from her garden. She is spiteful. I told Marian about it after and she laughed and said those two silly old lesbians.

I was dumb enough to ask what lesbians were instead of

looking it up in the dictionary and she said, "Oh, really! Don't you know *anything*?"

She said it's when women fall in love with each other and I said that's impossible, besides they are sister-in-laws. She said, "Honestly, how stupid can you get? What difference does that make? And it's sisters-in-law."

Then she said everybody has been talking about them for years and believe her, Dr. Pettigrew was no picnic when he was alive, either. She said, "Miss Pettigrew is a creep. Daddy says if she had been born two hundred years ago she would have been burned at the stake."

"You mean she's a witch?"

"No, dummy. I mean she doesn't conform."

"The whole thing is horrible," I said. "How could *anybody* love either Miss Pettigrew or Mrs. Pettigrew? Even each other?"

"That's lesbianism for you, kiddo," said Marian. "And speaking of queers, you're not doing so bad with that crazy old colonel of yours."

"He doesn't love anybody at all," I said. "And he's not crazy except for—" I stopped myself in time. "I concede that he has certain idiosyncracies."

"It's not pronounced 'i-dee-*aw*-sin-crass-ees'," she said, "and I still think your old Colonel is cuckoo."

It was my new word for the day from two weeks ago and I had been dying to use it. She would go and spoil it.

She's just jealous because she has never been allowed to see all the many treasures in the Colonel's house. She was hanging over the dinner table just as interested as He was when I told them about the carved lapis lazuli chess pieces and the wonderful toy soldiers. One of the toy soldier sets came from the grave of a grandson of Tamerlane—or was it Genghis Khan—in India. Anyway, the British got it when they looted his tomb, and it is made of white jade and gold. Another set is black jade, which in Chinese symbolizes ferocity.

Fatso said she didn't believe it but He said it was just possible, since the English have a habit of being very light fingered about treasure in other peoples' lands.

Take for example, He said, the Elgin Marbles. Even Marian didn't know what the Elgin Marbles were. It seems that a long time ago an Englishman named Lord Elgin carted away about half the Parthenon to the British Museum.

The Greeks are furious and want them returned but the English just smile and shake their heads.

The D I got in English was followed by my report card, which was a whole line of C-minuses and D's.

There was also a report from the school counselor that said I was withdrawn, shy, and uncooperative. She suggested I participate more in sports and attend the school dances.

I was absolutely aghast. To begin with, I hate sports and secondly I can't dance and I would just die if I had to face half the school at the dances, which are held in the gym.

Well, you don't tell Him that you *can't* do anything. He may tell you that you can't, but it doesn't work the other way around. After reading the report card and the letter He said I was going to the dance. I begged Him not to make me go and to strengthen my point I began to cry.

Marian said, "Cheer up, I'll ask Connor O'Rourke to dance with you."

My hair stood on end. "If she does," I shouted to Him, "I'll never speak to her again. I mean it!" And I did, too.

He turned to Marian and said, "That's enough of your horseplay. This letter says Isabel is withdrawn, shy, and un- cooperative and she's bloody well not going to be. I don't want any nonsense from you, or believe me it's you who will withdraw from society for a while."

Desperate, I said, "But I haven't anything to wear," which is the truth.

He didn't even look at me. He said to Marian, "Take her down to Park Royal and buy her a suitable dress."

We went the next afternoon. After trying on about a hundred, all of which looked like paper bags on my Bangladesh figure, I finally tried one on in black taffeta with a Peter Pan collar, puffed sleeves, and full gored skirt.

The salesgirl cried, "That's it! That's it! It's the newest style, a revival of the forties. The little-girl look!"

I didn't care one way or the other because I know the evening will be a dance Micawber in any case, but I thought maybe the real Anne might have had a dress like this so I said okay.

Marian is to take me and bring me home from the dance at eleven, which makes it two hours too long for me. It starts at nine.

Marian was very nice to me that night and did my hair for me and even said, "You know, you are very lucky to have such thick, naturally curly hair. I used to be jealous of it."

Then she stood back and looked at me and said, "I know just the thing!"

She went and got Mumma's two big tortoiseshell combs set with garnets that used to belong to Ann Carleon. She straightened the top of my hair and drew it back and set the combs in.

Then she stood back again and said, "You ought to have a corsage on black taffeta to make it look really elegant. Wait a minute."

She came back with Mumma's white cameo brooch, which she pinned on the front of my dress.

"There," she said. "You look perfect. Just like you're going to a state funeral or something."

He came in and stood looking at me.

"Well," I said, "how do I look?"

He turned to Marian.

"Are you sure that's what they're wearing now?"

"The salesgirl said it was the latest style."

"How do I look?" I said again.

"I don't know. Somewhere between a Spanish Infanta and Grandma Moses. Marian, do you know what the hell you're doing?"

She said yes, of course she did, and He went off mumbling to himself.

"Don't take any notice of Him," she said. "You know perfectly well that if He liked it, it would be hideous."

Which is quite true.

I will spare my readers all the horrors of that evening. Oh that this too too solid flesh would melt. The gym teacher came over and ordered me to join in the folk dancing and reels. Then the orchestra began to play regular music and I sat down. First someone came over and asked Marian and then another girl and another until there were only three of us left. I was shaking so much I put my hands between my knees and squeezed my knees together so nobody would notice.

Then the most terrible thing happened. I'd say it was just about the worst thing in my life, except that phrase is becoming threadbare in this diary.

I looked up as a shadow came between me and the dance

floor and there stood Connor O'Rourke. He is six feet tall and a football star. He looked down at me and said,

"Want to dance?"

And then!!!! Oh, my pen fails me!!! What demons possess me!!!???? I couldn't have stood up, let alone dance, so what did I do? I turned my head away haughtily and said, "Thank you, but I rarely dance with men."

I mean, what did I mean? I mean, honest, who else would I dance with? Did I mean I liked to dance with boys? Or girls? Or women? We will never know. All I know is I wished God would strike me dead.

He didn't, of course.

Conn O'Rourke just shrugged and smiled and said okay, then he went across the room and stood leaning against the wall. Every time I dared look at him he started to laugh. Maybe he smiled. I don't know. I always seem to look for the worst and it always happens. Maybe he was trying to be nice. I didn't wait around to find out.

I went into the girls' washroom and threw up. I stood in the cubicle with the door locked and leaned against the wall and shook.

Marian came in and banged on the door. "I know it's you, I can see your legs. You come out! You know what Daddy said. You've got to dance."

"Did you tell Conn O'Rourke to dance with me?" I asked between shudders.

"Did he?" she said.

"Yes, he did, and if you told him, I'm going to tell Him what you did and I will never forgive you and I'll kill you!" I said.

She said, oh, for heaven's sake, come out. She hadn't even spoken to Conn O'Rourke that evening and did I think she was dumb enough to do that and have to spend the rest of the year in the house, stupid?

Don't you see? This, if possible, makes it even worse.

"Well, you might as well come out because you have to stay until eleven o'clock," she said.

An hour and a half to go.

"I won't," I said.

Then the gym teacher came in and said, "Isabel McMurry, will you kindly come out of there and join the others?"

I said no, though I am not usually of a rebellious nature.

Then the student counselor came in and said, "Isabel, come out of there immediately."

I said no.

At eleven Marian came back and said, "Okay, you win. It's time to go back home."

It was the worst evening of my life. Touch wood. Every time I think things can't get worse, they do. I wonder if people make or control their destinies. If they do, I am sure doing a lousy job on mine.

The next day He didn't even ask about the dance or how I behaved. I guess he figured He had done his parental duty forcing me to go.

Fraser Schinbein has been given some sort of legal stay of prosecution and is out on bail if he will go to an institute in California that treats drug addicts. It is private and very expensive. Everybody is furious and is saying if the Schinbein's weren't so rich Fraser would be in the slammer so quick it would make your head swim. Even Marian says there seems to be one law for the rich and another for the poor and if you can afford a lawyer as prestigious as the Honorable Mr. Jay Thornton you can keep your kid out of jail forever, and if it were you or me we would be languishing in durance vile.

Marion's father was very amused by this observation and

said, "You can bet your bottom dollar you would, sweetheart, and I'd be the first to throw away the key."

The Misses Pettigrew nabbed me on the street yesterday.

Miss Pettigrew said, "You'll regret it, young lady. That wicked, wicked old man is dangerous."

Then Mrs. Pettigrew opened up her big mouth and said she couldn't imagine what my father could be thinking of.

They are mad. I mean mad-angry, because they hate the Colonel. They built a twelve-foot-high cedar wall between them and the Colonel's property. It's called a spite fence and it cut the morning sun off his rose garden.

The Colonel got out all his big guns and ammunition and prepared for battle. He carefully waited and watched while it was being built, then when it was finished he called his lawyer and the mayor, who called the Municipality, and the Pettigrews had to tear it down because it's against the zoning regulations to have a fence more than six feet tall, and of course that wasn't nearly high enough for them.

The Colonel was so jubilant, a lovely new word, isn't it? Sounds just like it means. When they had to tear it down he did a jig and cut an armful of roses for me to take home to Mumma. He never cuts his roses for people to put in flower vases ordinarily. He says it's brutal to cut them just any old way and they feel and bleed and wither if they are not pruned painlessly. He says it's the difference between an eighteenth-century field amputation and a heart transplant.

I brought the flowers home and Mumma was delighted. She put them in one of His Ming vases and I thought He would have a heart attack, but He managed to press His lips together and say nothing. When I told him what the Colonel said about roses suffering He said it was possible to be just a little too esoteric, but who was He to say. Personally, He believes the world is flat and those pictures we see of moon landings are only old Hollywood movies revamped. Also, He said, if He thought hard enough He could make his car run on water instead of gasoline, just like my Punjabi friend.

Later Marian said that as far as the water was concerned He probably thought He could walk on it.

I am very fortunate to have been adopted. They are all nuts.

Yesterday I told the Colonel how I prayed and prayed for God to make my mother better.

I said, "My doubts about God are getting very large." I also told him about my religious friend, Mrs. Lamb, and that so far nothing she has said has helped.

"What can I do? How can I find out?"

The Colonel sat staring into the fireplace in the billiard room, the hand that held his whiskey and soda trembling. For a time he didn't speak. Finally, without turning to me, he said,

"There is no God. Only ghosts and devils." Then he said if there were a God, wouldn't he know? Wouldn't he have seen God out in the desert at night, in the North African desert, which is like no desert in the world, where it's cold and clear and madmen think they can touch the stars?

And only madmen pray, he says, for they conjure up the Devil. Once, he said, he prayed and prayed all night long in the desert. The Devil heard him and came and the Devil was beautiful and beguiling beyond words.

But the Colonel was strong and resisted the Devil.

But not Carruthers. Carruthers was not strong. Carruthers listened to the Devil and was seduced by Him.

Carruthers became the Devil; the Devil's beauty Carruther's disguise.

It is all very puzzling.

I have been wondering lately if I am a lesbian. What I mean is, I love my sister-in-law. On the other hand I love Conn O'Rourke, too. It's very confusing and I wish I had someone to ask. Maybe Bonnie could straighten me out on it, although—I hate to come right out and say it—there are an awful lot of things Bonnie doesn't know anything about. I tried to tell her about the Colonel and the historic battles, but she just acted shocked and said,

"Do you mean to tell me your father *knows* you go over there and play with a dirty old man?"

Bonnie's got this thing about dirty old men. If she is really interested in D.O.M. she ought to get in touch with that master of bum pinchers, Professor Halden. I told her the Colonel was not a dirty old man and she said, yeah, when I was as old as her I would know they all were.

"Even Bud?" I asked, just out of meanness.

She turned to me and tears came to her eyes. She said,

"Isabel, that was very mean of you and you know it."

Sometimes I don't know what gets into me. "No, I don't," I said. "You said it, not me."

"Bud didn't have a mean bone in his body," she said and began to cry and I really did feel mean then. "He might have been kind of funny in some ways, like fighting on the wrong side, but he was the sweetest, kindest person in the whole world."

I guess he must have taken after my mother. I put my arms around Bonnie and told her I was sorry, and she dried her tears and said,

"I get so blue sometimes, Isabel, I mean Ann. You just wouldn't believe it. I'm so lonely and all the men I meet are after just one thing. Well, they won't get it from me. How will I ever meet anyone like Bud again?"

Yesterday was another beautiful day on the beach with the sailboats scudding in the bay and a brisk, sweet wind blowing. Definitely almost May Spoonish.

I should have known something would spoil it.

Peggy was lumbering back and forth in a frenzy of happiness, and so was I.

In the distance we could see the Italian workmen. They weren't spread out working on the seawall, but all huddled together on the beach, around something. The sea casts up strange things, and I wondered what it could be. You'd be surprised at some of the things I've picked up.

Primo turned around, saw me, waved and called, "Hey, come here! We gotta something for your dog."

We ran up, both of us panting. I couldn't see over their shoulders but Primo spoke to them in Italian and they all hooted with laughter, then he said again, "We gotta something for your dog."

They parted ranks and one called Fabreetsio, at least that's what it sounds like, suddenly lunged forward with something in his hands, and a big set of teeth snapped at Peggy. Peggy, who is the kindest dog in the world and who can't say boo to a goose, peed with fright and hobbled off with her tail between her legs and these guys all laughed like it was very funny.

The thing Fabreetsio was holding was absolutely horrible. It was a skull of some kind with holes where the eyes and ears and nose had been. The teeth were gray and big and very ugly. Fabreetsio clicked the jaws at me.

116

I jumped back and they all laughed again. Then Primo said, "Eh, eh!" to them, and still laughing, he took the skull, bowed and said, "For you, Seenyoreena."

I wanted to back off some more, but they had made me so mad scaring Peggy and then me that I wouldn't budge.

I said, trying to look very blasé, "What is that?"

Well, no one could think of it in English and they were all jabbering away in Italian, until one of them, named Vito said, "Baaa baaa baaa."

"A sheep," I said.

"See," said Primo. "That's eet. A ship."

I stood looking at it. I didn't know what I was supposed to do next. Primo said, "You want?"

Well of course I didn't want that rotten, ugly thing, but I wasn't going to let them make fun of Peggy and me and laugh at us and then think they had scared me so I said, "Sure. Why not?"

He gave it to me and after another round of laughs which made me even madder, they all went back to work.

I think grown-ups are rotten, particularly Italian grown-ups.

Anyway, there I was, standing there with this hideous rotten thing in my hands, sort of horrified at even holding it and wondering why I said I'd take it.

One thing was for sure. I couldn't leave it now, in front of them, so I walked off with it under my arm. It was quite heavy and big. About a mile farther on I sat on a log.

Peggy, who had been dogging, (huh, big laugh) my footsteps, came nearer and I called her over. She was very hesitant.

"It won't hurt you," I said. "I won't scare you like they did. It's all right. It won't bite you."

Finally, trembling all over (like me, she is very high-strung), she came right up and sniffed the skull.

After thinking it over, I decided to keep it in the box room. It's on the same floor as our bedrooms and is used to keep trunks and boxes and things. Along one side of it, with a door opening into the box room, is a long cupboard, about fourteen feet long and four wide. The floor there is unfinished and just has joists and plywood on it. The cupboard is used for all sorts of things that over the years nobody has wanted to throw away, plus the Christmas decorations. Everything is stored at the very far end of the closet, leaving about eight feet empty in the front.

The Christmas decorations are all carefully wrapped in tissue paper and packed in boxes. Some of them are very old, going back to my mother's childhood. There are tiny gold bird cages with even tinier gold birds in them, and glass robins, and swallows with spun-glass tails. There are beautiful tiny toy trumpets and bugles and fifes and flutes that really played tunes until *somebody* with very small sharp teeth chewed the blowing ends. A couple still work though, plus four tiny violins with real strings and bows that are always put at the very top of the tree now so that certain people can't gnaw them.

(It is my personal opinion that it was Bud, as he was the oldest, although who knows, it might even have been my mother or my Auntie Maude who went to Australia and was bitten by a spider.)

There are also some lovely little candles made of real wax that clip on the tree, which we have never been allowed to light because so many children have been killed by them in the past. "Little Willy dressed in sashes,/Fell in the fire and was burnt to ashes./ Suddenly the room grew chilly./ Nobody wanted to poke poor Willy." (Courtesy of my father to remind us never to play with fire.)

There are some gorgeous old glass balls that look grey until the light hits them—then they are all the colors of the rainbow. There are pink angels you can see through that have real little pink feathers for wings. You never see decorations like that any more.

There is one box with ropes of dried cranberries that are sort of mummified and hard as rocks, and a bunch of homemade decorations of cutout Santas and bells, paper chains and cotton glued onto clumsy little Hansel and Gretel houses that Bud and Marian and I made in kindergarten.

Fatso and I sit in the box room to read Aunt Ada's letters, but apart from that, nobody ever goes in there, especially the cupboard, from one Christmas to another.

I decided to keep the skull at the back of the closet, behind the Christmas decorations. You never know when something is going to come in handy, and it's too big to fit in Ann Carleon's little desk with my many other valuables.

I sat on the log wondering what I could do with it. People do make such interesting things with junk these days and sell them in the specialty shops in the village for a fortune. Last week I saw an old, solid-brass fire extinguisher that had been polished until it looked like gold. It had been made into a lamp and, would you believe it, cost five hundred dollars. Somebody else had taken an old hand pump, the kind you see on TV in farm kitchens, and made a lamp from it and it cost *six* hundred dollars. I don't know why people pay money like that for old things, but they do, at least in West Vancouver. In one of the antique shops there was a thing called a dry sink, which is just an old tin sink set in a cupboard, with a chamber pot in the sink part, filled with artificial flowers, and you just wouldn't believe what they wanted for that.

The more I thought about the skull, the more interesting it

became. A bird feeder? A table lamp? A candleholder? Split it in two and make bookends? A hanging planter? The possibilities are endless and quite exciting.

On my way back I had to pass the men. I had figured it out before I left that log, thanks to the Colonel and his lessons in strategy. I have, after all, been taught by a master.

I had the skull under my left arm, but with my right hand I gave them a small, stiff backward wave, just like the Queen does when she is in her state carriage, and I bowed my head very slightly, just like she does. I did not smile; instead, I walked very gravely past them, like royalty.

I half expected them to start shouting in Italian and laughing, but they didn't, so I looked back. They were all standing there with their trowels and hammers in midair, like one of those old-fashioned Victorian pictures where people look like statues. They stared at me as if I were nuts.

My second line of attack (the Colonel's advice): surprise.

I stuck my tongue out at them, laughed like a hyena, and ran the rest of the way down the beach yelling "Geronimo!"

It serves them right. They all looked terrified. Besides, if they are going to think I am crazy, they might as well think I am good and loony.

Oh, my pen fails me! The most awful news three days ago. Fraser Schinbein is dead, snatched to the tomb in the bloom of his youth.

He had just come back from that private drug rehabilitation center in California and the Schinbeins gave a big family party to celebrate his return all safe and sound and drug-free.

He could probably get a suspended sentence now, they thought, and they were all very happy.

Well, after the party, when his keeper, a male nurse who had been looking after him, went home, Fraser went up to his room. And, as Marian says, shot it up. Heroin.

Marian explained to me that he had lost all his tolerance for the drug after being at the California center. He took the same amount he used to, and he died from an overdose. Nobody can figure out how or where he got the heroin, as he was watched night and day.

Marian did not go to the funeral. He was buried the next day, which seemed sort of rushing things to me, but Marian says that's how Jewish people do it. It's got something to do with sundown.

The newspapers ran the story on the front page and even had a TV newscast of the funeral.

Later Rhea told Marian that it is the most awful thing for her poor parents, who will never get over it. Rhea said that it is the most terrible thing in the whole world for a Jewish family. A son, and particularly an only son, is the most important member of the family and we couldn't possibly imagine how awful it is for them.

This offended me deeply. I mean, who is Rhea to say how we feel, and what right has she to assume that we didn't care when Bud died? It made it sound as if they loved Fraser and we didn't love Bud.

I cannot remember much about Bud, but I am sure if he had lived I would have been very fond of him. Mumma certainly was.

About the only very clear memory I have of Bud is of me sitting on the front steps crying and Bud giving me his cigarette to smoke and cheer me up. I don't know if it cheered me up, but it did make me throw up, and I remember somebody shouting, "I *told* you she would!"

Any way you look at it, I think Fraser Schinbein asked for it. As far as I can see, he didn't care for anybody but himself. Marian said that if he cared for himself he would not have treated his body like a pincushion and that he must have been deeply disturbed and let it be a lesson to me what can happen to people who smoke pot. I said I didn't smoke pot and anyway, he died from heroin by her very old testimony, and she said if he hadn't started on pot he wouldn't have gone on to hard drugs. Anyway, as far as I'm concerned, I really don't care if he died sticking beans up his nose. All I am really thinking about is his poor fiancée, Jane Lonsdale. Oh, how that shattered girl must be grieving.

As I said to Marian, "Oh, who sits weeping on my grave, and will not let me rest?"

And Marian said, "Oh, quit *wallowing* in other people's woes!"

Naomi looked very withdrawn at school, but since I don't ordinarily talk to her I didn't see any point in being a hypocrite and going over and saying I was sorry about her brother when I'm not. Besides, Marian would probably accuse me of *wallowing*.

Well, you can't win. Marion says I should have offered my condolences even if I hated Fraser Schinbein, which I certainly didn't.

Now I am worried that Naomi Schinbein will think I didn't speak because of her not voting for me in the Camorras, but as God is my witness that has nothing to do with it, although I don't suppose Marian would believe me.

I'm getting awfully lazy about keeping my diary. Nothing ever happens, but I suppose you can't expect thrilling, I mean chilling, tragedy like Fraser Schinbein every day.

Although it's only days, it seems like ages since I have been to the beach. I went today and Primo and the gang were all working hard and looking down as if they didn't see me. I was nearly past them when Primo called me.

"Mees!" He came forward with a small package wrapped in fancy paper in his hand.

"No see you. You seek? You take thees."

I didn't want any more of their crummy presents and I could hardly do my royalty act again, when I noticed the men were all looking, or rather, not looking, at me in a funny kind of way. Sort of furtive. Almost as if they were ashamed.

"Please," said Primo. "You take."

He patted Peggy's head and said, "Nice, your dog, eh?"

Well, I took the parcel. I didn't open it then in case it was another of their lousy jokes. When I walked back, past them, I held it so they could see I had not yet deigned to open it.

The Colonel always says keep 'em guessing, girl, so I did. They all cast sidelong looks, so I nodded and gave them the smallest smile anybody could possibly give.

They started really smiling, quite nicely this time. I guess Italians aren't so bad. They all have beautiful teeth.

When I got home, I opened the package. It was a box of candied violets.

People sure are funny. The violets taste awful and even Fatso wouldn't eat them, so I put them in with my many treasures as a memento.

I must remember to make out a will.

I had tea yesterday afternoon with my religious friend, Mrs. Lamb. She has been asking me to her house for ages, but I have been kind of cheesed off with religion recently. She lives across the bridge, way over at the other end of Vancouver. I had to take four buses to get there and was I scared. I was sure I'd never find the place, but the bus drivers were very kind. One of them even got out of his bus after I got off and took me across the street. It seems I was waiting at a bus stop on the wrong side. Anyhow, after many adventures and heart-stopping frights, I got off the last bus in a run-down district lined with mean little houses. Mrs. Lamb's house and garden were neat—as a matter of fact they all were—but they were just the sort of houses you couldn't do anything with to improve, except maybe keep neat.

When she invited me in I got a shock because the furniture was so old and shabby. Now I know what Bonnie means about our house.

Everything looked like it came from a Salvation Army thrift shop. There was a tatty old grayish-pink chesterfield sofa covered in a nubby material worn to the threads. They also had a green, shaky-looking armchair with a big dent in the seat where the springs were broken, and an old gray-green rug about as thick as a bath towel. There were no end tables or coffee tables, just a barrel cut in half with a piece of varnished plywood on it. They had no fireplace, ornaments, light fixtures, lamps, books, or flowers. They did have a big picture of Jesus with his eyes turned up showing the whites, and his hand holding his bleeding heart against his chest. It was a room I can only describe as *barren,* although it wasn't the barrenness or poorness of everything that got to me.

It was a sort of braveness. I really can't describe it.

The biggest shock, though, was Mr. Lamb.

He was in a wheelchair and he had no legs.

Although I hope I didn't show it, I was horrified.

As if he read my thoughts, he said, "Don't let me frighten you, my dear. I am a diabetic and I have had my legs amputated."

Mrs. Lamb said, "Dad always believes in telling young people the truth and they always understand. They've never let you down yet, have they, Dad?"

He said no and she asked if I had any trouble finding the place. I was going to lie as usual and say no, but I was still not too sure about this God business and if He were listening it sure wouldn't look too good telling a lie as soon as I got in the front door. I said I had had a little difficulty but fortunately was able to overcome it.

"That's right, my dear. I'll wager you said a little prayer, didn't you?"

Well, even if God was listening, I couldn't say no so I said yes.

We talked about one thing and another, and then she asked about school. I thought they'd get right into religion, but they didn't. I told them about the dance. I was going to say only that I'd been to one, but I never can keep my big mouth shut once I get started and before I knew it I had told them the whole ghastly story.

She and Mr. Lamb nodded as if it were the most terrible and important event in the whole world.

Then Mr. Lamb said, "My dear, I always used to worry and expect the worst, and it always happened, until one day I realized I was not living my religion. Then I *gave* myself to God and my whole life has changed, the Lord be praised, and now I expect the best and that is what I get!"

He then went on about how he was filled with a great and

tremendous happiness and he actually said he wanted to get down on his knees and thank sweet Jesus for his bounty and mercy.

Well, that was too much for me. I mean, I just don't know. If the best Jesus can do is cut off both your legs and then make you feel you ought to get down on what you haven't got in thanks, then I don't want any part of it. I may as well also be completely honest and say that I don't want to be poor and live in a squalid little house filled with ugly furniture.

I didn't say anything or look different during all this. I don't know if it's because I'm a natural hypocrite, but I just couldn't argue about their religion and I couldn't even think, let alone speak about his legs.

Instead, I asked about their children. They don't have any. I thought that because she called him Dad, they would.

Mrs. Lamb said, "No, though we always wanted children, Jesus saw fit to give us other responsibilities."

There you go again, see?

Mr. Lamb broke in. "You see, Isabel, it's a matter of compensation. Instead of having children of our own, we are privileged to save the children of others. Now which do you think would please our Lord most?"

I had no opinion on the subject so I just smiled and said oh.

Mrs. Lamb made tea and we had tuna sandwiches and homemade diabetic cookies and Marian said later that I probably ate their food supply for a week. You see, the Lord in his wisdom, apart from everything else, has seen fit to let them live on a very small disability pension.

Mrs. Lamb must have read my mind because she said that their needs were small and what they had was sufficient and that Jesus had never failed to provide.

"It's the bread and the fishes story, time and again, Isabel. Time and again."

I was really beginning to understand what Bonnie is always harping on, about how lucky Marian and I are. I really *will* stop my beefing. Here were these two old people with so little and yet uncomplaining. At least, I guess they were old. After people get to a certain age and have gray hair and false teeth they all look pretty much the same to me.

Their happiness should have made me believe in God, but I felt strange; something was wrong somewhere, but I couldn't put my finger on it.

Just when I was beginning to relax and sort of forget the awfulness of their lives, they, as the Colonel would say, brought out their big guns.

And believe me, they've got the biggest gun in the world and it's called Armageddon. It's the end of the world and the second coming of the Messiah, who, much to my surprise, turns out to be Jesus. Only the just, no, that's not right, only the Just, who have lived purely and who believe in Him, will be saved from the Terror.

It gets very complicated, but I'll try to remember. Just before He comes, there will be a false prophet in the east, and a king of Rome and a false Messiah in the west, or maybe it's the other way around, and Gog, who comes out of Russia, and the hordes of Asia, are all going to sweep across the world and meet in Armageddon, which is in Israel. Then the Unjust are going to go up like a bunch of Roman candles. That isn't how they put it, because they quoted the Bible, but it's something about everything except the Just being scorched and burnt. It really describes nuclear warfare, Mr. Lamb said.

Mr. Lamb sat there in his wheelchair with his poor old thin, spotted hands waving and trembling with excitement, and Mrs. Lamb's face seemed to glow.

I felt there was something terribly wrong. People with as many things to cope with as they have, *shouldn't* be happy. I mean, what have they got to be happy about? It's not natural.

After they tapered down about this end of the world business they said I was very young and it might take me some time to absorb the immensity of the Message and that we would talk about it again.

They asked me to visit soon and I said I would because I can't say no, and Mrs. Lamb said,

"Dad just loves having young people around, and you are my first contact in West Vancouver, and I can't tell you how much it means to me. My dear, West Vancouver is the Sodom and Gomorrah of British Columbia. But as Scripture says, a little child shall lead them all."

Mr. Lamb said "Hallelujah" and looked very happy and I felt like a great big fibber. I just *know* I can't go back to their place.

When I got home it sure looked good. I got to thinking that the miracle is they are happy when they haven't got anything to be happy about, except being among the Just.

So here I am, right back where I started, wanting miracles, seeing miracles, and not believing in miracles.

I don't know if it was seeing the Lambs, but when I got home I just couldn't eat. The food simply stuck in my throat. I am now two hundred pounds underweight, and just to complicate things, Marian decided tonight to go on a diet. She doesn't need to, because she's not really fat. I just call her that to bug her. Her excuse for dieting is that you can't be too rich or too thin. Poor girl, little does she know.

Well, with both of us not eating tonight it made Him go absolute ape, and we both got the full range of the old Bangladesh routine, which I have to admit has lost its effect on me. We both just sat there and stared at him with what he calls "dumb insolence," so He exploded with what Marian refers to as his blue-plate special, the old "I have made of my realm a second Africa, fertile only in monsters."

Then he banged his fist on the table so that all the plates jumped up and down and shouted, "Well, all right then! All right! Leave my table! Both of you! Go to your rooms! Starve! Damn you, starve!"

Since neither of us wanted to eat anyway, it was no great hardship. We went to our rooms.

Neither of us were there for breakfast the next morning. He shouted upstairs,

"Marian! Isabel! Where the hell are you? It's nearly half past eight! Get down here and eat your breakfasts or you'll be late for school."

So we did. All I wanted to eat was tea and toast, but to avoid a fight I had an egg as well. Fatso had made up her mind she would have unsweetened tea and dry toast. She ended up having grapefruit, cereal, bacon, eggs, and toast with Him.

He never said a word about the night before.

Ho hum.

Bonnie was waiting for me when I got out of school. "Hop in," she said. "We'll drive down to Ambleside and watch the sailboats."

When we got to Ambleside she offered me a stick of gum, then she lit a cigarette and sat staring out the car window at the sailboats.

"Would you like to get out and walk on the beach?" I asked. She shook her head.

"I'd rather just sit. Listen, do you remember I told you I was going to the police about that pervert?"

My heart skipped a beat.

"Well, they said they couldn't do anything about him unless you identified him and I refused to give your name."

"Whew!" I said with relief.

"Well, that wasn't the end of it. I mean—"

She paused.

"Can I have a puff?" I asked. "No," she said. "It'll stunt your growth and give you lung cancer."

I have been, as usual, the author of my own destruction, or misfortune, or whatever it is.

She sat there telling me how she met this policeman and he asked her out and they have seen a lot of each other. And how he has asked her to marry him.

"Oh, no!" I cried. "Bonnie! You couldn't do that! You just couldn't! You said you'd never marry again! You did! You know you did!"

"People can change their minds," she said. "Don't you want me to be happy?"

I began to cry.

"Why are you crying? I thought you'd be happy for me. Don't you want me to be happy?"

"No," I said, "not if it means everything's changed."

"Nothing will change, you silly goose," she said, and put her arm around me.

"Yes it will!" I said.

"What will?" she said.

"You'll like him better than me."

"I will not. Don't be silly. We'll be just like we always are. And in a few years, before you know it, you'll be on your own and can come and visit me whenever you want. How about that?"

I couldn't stop crying. Why do things always have to change?

"Now stop it," she said. "He's one hell of a swell guy and I know you're going to like him."

"I *HATE* him," I said.

She laughed. "You're just as pigheaded as Bud. Bernie is one of the finest people I have ever known and I know you are going to like him just as much as I do."

"Why do you have to marry him?" I cried. "Why can't you just live in sin like Lady Isabel Vane? Then you can leave him if you feel like it!"

She gave me a Kleenex and told me to blow my nose.

"Now that's enough," she said. "We'll go on being best friends just as we always have been and I'll meet you after school just like I always do and you won't even know the difference. You'll like him, I know."

Before I could answer, she suddenly went a funny color and got out of the car and threw up.

"Oh, Bonnie!" I got out, too, and put my arms around her as she bent over. "Oh, Bonnie! Are you still sick? I'm sorry, honest I am. I'll be good. I'll quit being the limit, honestly, I will."

"Hand me a Kleenex from my purse."

I did and she wiped her mouth and straightened up.

"I'm all right. I just can't seem to shake this damn flu."

She let me off a couple of blocks from home.

I feel even rottener than usual. Why are things always changing?

It's awful being all alone and having no friends. For instance, I can't even go to the show on Saturday night. I'm not going to wait in line all by myself and then walk in front of everybody and sit by myself while everybody else is with somebody else. I can't even go to the Dairy Queen for a milk shake when I have the money because that's where all the Camorras hang out and I would die of pride or fright before I would walk in there all by myself.

Today I was so depressed about Bonnie's wedding—it means I will *have no one at all*—that I decided to phone her, just to talk to another human being and see if she was feeling better.

There is a pay phone on the sidewalk right outside the Dairy Queen. I put my money in it and it rang and rang and rang but there was no answer. It seemed as if the whole world was against me and there was a feeling like lead in my throat. My lips began to tremble and tears rolled down my face.

Somebody tapped on the glass door with a coin. I didn't turn and they tapped again. I had hung up and I guess they wanted to use the phone. Finally I turned around and opened the door.

There stood the most wonderful-looking person in the world.

He seemed to be made of gold. His clothes were pale beige suede, his skin was a pale gold, his hair was bright gold, and his eyes were the color of honey. His shirt was open and around his neck he wore a heavy gold chain. He wore a gold watch on one wrist, a golden bracelet on the other, and a golden ring on his right hand, set with a huge diamond. He looked like a god from ancient times.

When he saw the tears raining down my face he took a step back.

"I didn't mean to upset you *that* much," he said.

So he was human, and could speak just like us.

"I can wait," he said. "Go ahead. Complete your call."

"It's over," I said.

He looked at me for a minute and said, "I'm sure it can't be as bad as all that. Things seldom are."

Ordinarily I don't go around blubbering to strangers, but grief made me reckless. Besides, he wasn't like other human beings.

"You're wrong," I said through my tears. "Not only are they as bad as that, they're worse. They always are, and what's more, they are getting worser all the time and they are going to keep getting worser."

"You know what I think?" he said. "I think you need a drink. How about a soda in there?"

I was going to say, oh, no, not in there, but then I realized I wouldn't be alone! I could hardly believe my ears. "You mean it?" I said.

"Bless my soul, you are almost as suspicious as myself," he said. "Come on, I won't bite you."

"Okay," I said, so in front of all those Camorras we marched into the Dairy Queen. We sat in a sort of alcove at the back, away from everybody else, but I heard a murmur go over all the Camorras as we walked past them, me with tears still rolling down my face.

He ordered two chocolate sodas and sat opposite me. Then he said for me to tell him everything.

"Everything?" I said.

"Everything," he said. "Spare me nothing and trust me in all."

So I told him about my sister-in-law getting married, about Miss Swanson, and the beach and the mountains and how things kept changing, and about Fraser Shinbein killing himself with drugs. Actually, the way I went on, you would have thought that I, instead of Jane Lonsdale, was engaged to him, but the absolute tragedy of my life kind of swept me along.

He sat for a while thinking and then he said, "Wait a minute. You've lost me somewhere. You're crying because your sister-in-law is getting married, right? But how can your sister-in-law get married if she is married to your brother?"

I told him Bud was dead.

"Dead?"

"Yes," I said. "In the Vietnam War."

"I am sorry to hear that. It was a stupid war."

"Yes," I said. "That's what Bonnie says. She says Bud was stupid, too."

He looked rather surprised. "She does?" He said. "How come?"

"Well, because he was captured by South Vietnamese peasants."

"South Vietnamese? Wasn't he on the wrong side?"

"Well, that's what Bonnie says, too. No one in our house ever talks about him. Never. I myself never think of him."

"That's very strange," he said. "Why?"

I told him how Bud died.

His golden skin suddenly went yellow. He put his hand over mine and said, "*Oh, God!*" Then he sighed and asked, "What's your name?"

I said Ann Carleon, which was sort of dumb because there on the table was my math notebook with Isabel McMurry printed right on top of it in big letters. He asked me if I lived in West Van and I said only temporarily. I told him that my family was Hungarian, but they had been split up before my birth during the revolution and I had been trying to find them.

He said Carleon didn't sound very Hungarian and I said actually I was Italian on my father's side and that we were related to the Corleones of *The Godfather*. I had stopped crying and was now beginning to enjoy myself.

He squeezed my hand and said I reminded him of a boy he once knew.

"Where is he now?" I asked.

"Oh, he grew up, but I keep running into him in unexpected places. It's funny, you being foreign, too. You undoubtedly are a Hapsburg who was kidnapped during infancy."

For a minute I was puzzled, then I remembered who the Hapsburgs were because I watched *Meyerling* on TV.

"I myself am a Romanov," he said and printed it on a napkin. Even his pen was gold. There it was: Alexis Romanov.

He leaned over to me. "This must be our secret. The Tsar's family did not all die in 1918. The Tsarevitch, the rightful heir to all the Russias, escaped, though very few know about it. I am his lawful son and heir." He beckoned me even closer and whispered, "There are millions of rubles deposited in a Swiss bank for me as soon as I can prove my inheritance."

"No kidding?" I said.

"Yup. Just got to prove it and it's all mine."

I looked out the window. There was a big gold Mercedes Benz parked at the curb.

"Is that your car?" I asked.

He nodded.

"You look as if you're doing okay now," I said.

He laughed.

"A mere drop in the bucket, my dear Miss Carleon. How I wish you could have seen the imperial jewels. Among them, mere baubles, were the Orlov Diamond at 194 carats, the Moon of the Mountain, an uncut diamond of about 120 carats, and the most beautiful of them all—a magnificent, huge ruby called the Polar Star. And the sapphires! Forgive me, but even *your* eyes would pale beside them."

"Would you mind writing down their names and weights?"

He added that to his writing on the paper napkin.

I wanted to remember because the very names of the jewels thrilled me. I mean, imagine stones having names! The Polar

Star. Just the sound of it made a chill run down my spine.

"I tell you, Ann, if I had come into my inheritance, that glass of ice cream and soda would be filled with emeralds, as just a small gesture of my pleasure of your company. Really, it's rotten not being even a Grand Duke, I, who should have been the Tsarevitch and eventually Tsar of all the Russias."

I really didn't know what to say.

He opened my math book and there it was again, that dumb Isabel McMurry, Division 84.

"McMurry," he said. "That name rings a bell. Ah yes, the name of those peasants who adopted you."

I nodded. He and I were made for each other.

"Say, Ann," he said, "Would you by any chance be related to that cybernetics nut, Charles McMurry? I heard he lived over here."

I admitted we were distantly related.

He said how refreshing it was to meet one of his own after these many years.

And then, oh, then, he looked at his gold watch and said, "Good grief! It's after two and I have a meeting with my board in town in ten minutes!"

He stood up, bowed from the waist, lifted my hand, kissed it and said, "Farewell, Ann, not good-bye. I know we are destined to meet again."

It was like watching the sun sink to see him go outside and jump into his golden car.

All the Camorras came crowding around me. "Gee, who was he?" "Who's that?" "Where did you meet him?"

Then that snake in the grass, that son of a bitch Beatrice said, "Why were you crying?"

Even in the sorrow of parting so soon, it was my moment of triumph.

Ann Landers would have been proud of me.

"His wife won't give him a divorce because of the children," I said.

I keep the napkin with the writing written in his princely hand. I keep it in my desk between sheets of tissue paper, next to my embroidery.

I wish I had a photograph of him. I have thought of him so much but sometimes I can't recall his face.

Parting is not such sweet sorrow. I haven't written for days. Today my word is obduracy. Impenitent, hard, callous, insensible. Like most people. Oh, if only I could just see him again, even from a distance. I may as well face the fact. I no longer love Conn O'Rourke.

It's ages since I have seen Bonnie. I wanted to see her to tell her about him, but she is never in. I wish I could keep a secret, but I just can't. Half the fun of knowing something is telling someone. I phoned again and this time I got her in.

She said she was pretty busy but when she got time she'd call and make arrangements to meet me after school. It was eons before she did and it just about killed me not being able to talk to anyone about Mr. Romanov.

I had completely forgotten I had promised not to run around with strange men.

When I told her about him she didn't get mad like she did about the guy at the beach, which proves that she doesn't care about me as she used to.

She just shrugged and said, "Oh, really, Isabel, you are the limit. I am wasting my time. I might as well talk to a door."

If she really cared about me she would have got mad.

She laughed when I told her what I said to Beatrice. She didn't even seem very impressed by Mr. Romanov, but then, of course, she didn't see him.

She just said, "How are things at home? How is your mother?"

"Everything's just the same," I said.

Then I remembered about the redecorating. There are workmen all over the place in his upstairs part of the house. Considering we're so poor it doesn't make sense but then, in our house, what does? I tried to sneak up and have a look and see what it's like but He caught me and sent me downstairs.

When I told Bonnie she just sniffed and said, "It's nothing special up there—just walls and walls of books and big maps everywhere with colored pins stuck in them, and filing cabinets."

I looked at her in amazement.

"But how do you know?" I said.

Her face went kind of red and she said forget it.

"Have you been up there?" I asked. "How come? Nobody but Him was ever up there."

"I said forget it!" She sounded mad, although I don't know why. She didn't get mad about Mr. Romanov.

"Okay," I said, "I just don't understand."

"Look," she said, "it was a slip of the tongue and believe me, it didn't mean anything."

Then she looked right into my eyes. "Don't you tell anyone I was up there. Do you hear me?"

"Sure, Bonnie, but—" She cut me short again.

"Now you promise me you won't, particularly to your mother or Marian."

"As if I tell old Blabbermouth anything," I said.

"She's not the only old Blabbermouth in your family. Swear on Bud's memory."

"Aw, gee, Bonnie," I said, "don't make me do that. What if I was tortured? I'd tell anything, anything, if somebody just twisted my arm."

"Okay," she said. "Swear on your word of honor and cross your heart." So I did and then I said, "But when were you up there? Was it before or after Bud died?"

"Before, of course!" she sort of screamed. "Do you think I'd go up after?"

I don't know why she was so mad at me. I hadn't done anything, except to go out with another strange man and she didn't care about that. Bonnie has been awfully short-tempered lately.

Then she sort of relented and said, "Like I said, it was no big deal. Nothing happened or I wouldn't have blurted it out. Bud laughed like hell when I told him. You'll find this hard to believe, Isabel. No, you won't find this hard to believe, knowing your father, but He ended up giving me a lecture about the Pope. The *Pope*, for crying out loud, and I'm not even a Catholic. Bud said it served me right for being dumb enough to be *talked* into going up there. Bud said the Irish can talk you into anything. Anyway, He was ranting and raving about how, if the Pope had excommunicated all the German and Italian Catholics for committing atrocities, thirty million lives could have been saved. I left when he started on about the six million Jews and you know what He's like about *that*."

I sure did. The way He carries on about them you'd think He was Jewish, which is a pity He isn't, because then I'd be half Jewish and I'd kind of like that.

"Why is it all right that you told Bud but I can't tell Mumma or Marian?"

"Bud understood *everything*, you little twerp." Then she hugged me.

Bonnie doesn't look good. As a matter of fact she looks rotten. Maybe that's why she's been so cranky lately. Maybe she is sick. I should have asked her but she probably wouldn't have told me. Nobody ever tells me anything.

Ages as it is, it seems like only yesterday that I met Mr. Romanov. I keep searching for him. Wherever I go in West Vancouver, which isn't very big, I look for him.

Well, as Uncle Billy would say, today was a son of a bitch even by my standards.

I went down to the Mall in Park Royal. Several days ago I received a phone call from Mrs. Lamb saying that religious canvassing is forbidden in the Mall now and asking me when I could visit. I lied as usual and said soon, but I was awfully relieved to hear that she won't be at Park Royal anymore because I am afraid of meeting her and if she asked me face-to-face to visit her, I would promise it and really mean it and have to do it. It's a lot easier lying over the phone.

I was by myself (naturally), when I saw him: the Golden One. I could hardly believe my luck. My heart started to pound. It was very crowded and I ran hither and thither toward him among the people. When I reached him and caught his arm he turned and looked down at me.

It wasn't him at all. It was just a fellow wearing a yellow suede jacket.

I said I was sorry. Tears came to my eyes and my lips began to tremble. "I thought you were somebody else," I said.

He laughed and he looked sort of embarrassed. He said, "I think what you really mean is you *hoped* I was somebody else."

That hit the nail right on the head.

We parted without a regret or a backward glance.

I walked away and sat on a bench. If only it had been him. I know just how it would have been. He would have clasped me to his heart and said, "Ann! My terrible search has ended! We shall never, never be parted again!"

Then we would have gone into the Swiss Conditorei Restaurant in the Mall and sat opposite each other at a small table with a white cloth and a single red, red rose in a crystal stem vase.

Between tears we would hold hands. He would order coffee and I would have a milk shake and Black Forest cake, which costs a dollar fifty for a slice not much wider than your finger.

"We must run away, my beloved. There is no other solution."

He has a slight Viennese accent I never noticed before.

"But where can we flee?"

He squeezes my hand with his strong brown one.

"To my castle, high in the Alps, my darling, where else? There we shall be safe."

His castle, which is called Rosenwald (courtesy of the *National Geographic*), is very beautiful.

"Did you see *The Sound of Music*?" he asks. "My castle is just like that only much bigger and better. I have dungeons, a polo ground, a miniature railroad, a Swedish sauna—you name it and I've got it."

Life at the castle is very gracious. I generally wear a long white dress in the evenings, with ostrich feathers in my hair. Our guests are mostly royalty and my favorite movie stars, but we only bring out the solid-gold dishes for Queen Elizabeth, as they would get dented if we used them every night.

We live there alone, except, of course, for our seventy-eight servants. Our gardens are even better than the Colonel's and I spend a great deal of my time picking roses, the best of which I use to adorn my hair, behind my tiara. Our chef has a sweet tooth so we live largely on spun-sugar delights and chocolate cake, although he is fortunately partial to French fries and hamburgers as well, so our diet is well balanced.

There is a big wall around the castle and nobody gets in without an invitation, especially my family, and particularly my mean old adopted father, although the Prince demurred at this.

"I think, my dearest, that on state occasions you ought to ask them, for the sake of appearances."

And so, on my birthday and state holidays, etc., we have them all over for dinner. (Peggy lives with me in the castle all the time, of course.)

My family is terribly impressed. Marian hardly dares open her mouth and stops correcting people's English and offering advice and my father, as He bows over my hand, says,

"Well, I never would have thought you had it in you, Your Serene Highness."

Mother, who is very healthy, runs delightedly from room to room, exclaiming on the many treasures therein.

My daydream ended with a rotten, aching jolt. It was old Fatso, also wandering around the Mall unbeknownst to me, and she poked me in the ribs.

"Are you asleep or crazy or something, sitting there in public with your eyes closed and your lips moving? You look like some kind of idiot!"

"Oh, shut up!" I said. "Go away."

What's the use? I hope I am not going to go through life thinking I am catching a glimpse of him, then rushing up to find a complete stranger. And what is even worse, look how I act with Conn O'Rourke. I just walk right past him like I don't know him. Of course, that is what I always did with him. After today I suppose that's what I'll do if I see Alexis Romanov. I am so stupid.

Oh, well, things could be worse. Look what happened to the real Anne. And then there's Bonnie. How awful it must have been for her when Bud died.

Poor Bonnie. She could never have built herself an imaginary castle all her own to retire to when she was utterly despairing.

I have been thinking more and more about Mr. Romanov and the more I think the more I want to know more about him.

I went to my father. "Do you have any books on the Russian royal family?" I asked.

"Russia hasn't got a royal family. It's a communist country. Don't they teach you anything at that school?"

"I mean in the olden days, before the revolution. I mean about a family who were called the Romanovs and were Tsars."

He looked down at me with surprise. Then He said, "Yes, as a matter of fact I have some excellent ones. Would you like to read them?"

I said yes, so He went upstairs and came down with three. There was a big one called *Nicholas and Alexandra*, and one called *Once a Grand Duke* by Grand Duke Alexander, and one called *Lost Splendors* by Prince Felix Yousoupoff.

Well, it's been three weeks since I have written in my diary and I have finally finished the books. And there isn't much I don't know about the Russian royal family, even if I am a dud in Latin and English and math and a few other subjects. It is absolutely fascinating and I sort of hated to finish the last book. I honestly and really *should* have been born into royalty.

I was in the den where He and Marian and Mumma were watching television.

"Could the Tsarevitch have got away?" I asked him.

"Not now!" Marian said. "Why do you always have to talk at the *crucial* point! Go away!"

I opened my mouth but she hissed like a serpent so He got up and led me to the dining room.

He looked very pleased that I was interested in Russian royalty, although I really guess he was pleased that I was interested in anything.

"No," He said. "I don't think the Tsarevitch could have escaped."

"The books don't either."

He nodded. "Why do you care? It all happened so long ago."

"I find history very fascinating," I said. "Did you see the pictures of him in the books?"

"Who?" He said.

"The Tsarevitch," I said.

"Ah, yes," He said. "He was a remarkably beautiful child. As a matter of fact, considering they were as inbred as Berkshire hogs, they were a handsome family."

"And he couldn't have got away?"

He shook his head. "I doubt it. The evidence was pretty conclusive. The White Army didn't miss much sifting through the ashes. Jewels, teeth, belt buckles, corset stays, monogrammed buttons."

I shuddered.

"He would have died anyway, you know. He was a royal

bleeder and probably wouldn't have lived out his teens. Most of them haven't."

He took my face between his hands and stood looking down at me for a long time. He does that sometimes. I think He is looking for Bud.

"And on the walls of that cellar where they were shot was written, 'And in the night Balthazar was murdered by his slaves.' "

He still stood with my face in his hand, looking down at me. "Heine wrote that. He was a German Jew."

He chucked me under the chin. "Run along and play now."

He went back to watch television and I went upstairs to my room to talk to the real Anne.

They were all wrong. All the writers, all the historians, and especially Him.

The Tsarevitch escaped. He must have. He was only fourteen. How could he die?

But they did kill my friend, the real Anne, and she wasn't much older.

It makes me feel strange. Once I thought I would live forever. Now I'm not even sure I'll grow up.

I *know* the two girls in the hospital knew they were going to die, and even when the doctors thought I was bleeding to death from my throat, I *knew* I wasn't. I wouldn't be so sure now. I wonder if Bud knew he was going to die.

Bonnie once said he might just as well have stayed home and put a revolver against his temple. She says it would have been quicker and less trouble for everybody especially her.

A real field day today! I saw Lady Clementine, the Black Rose. The Colonel had promised me I could see her when she was ready and today he let me into the greenhouse.

I thought that he would be transplanting Lady Clementine out of the greenhouse; at least, that's how I interpreted his statement that he would have to get her out in the air, but that's not what he's going to do at all. He is going to dismantle the greenhouse around her.

I must admit to being rather disappointed when I saw Lady Clementine. For all that he says she is black, she is definitely not. She is *almost* black but you can still see, where the light hits her petals, a deep murky purple. Apart from that she is really a very nice-looking rose. About my height, maybe a little shorter, not very bushy, with one bloom fully developed but not yet open, and several buds.

Of course, I did not let the Colonel know she looks pretty much like any other rose and I tried to sound as if he had created a treasure, but really, to tell the truth, she hasn't even got much scent. She is not even close to my favorite, the Montgomery Gore, for instance.

Last night we sat up and watched a movie on TV about Charlton Heston leading the Israelites out of Egypt. It was a super movie, particularly the part where Charlton Heston got the Ten Commandments on the mountain, and God said in this very deep, scary voice, "Take off thy shoes, for the ground you stand on is holy ground," or something like that. Then there was this really keen scene where the Israelites built a golden calf. They put flowers around its neck and had an orgy and danced and sang around it. This made Moses and God so mad that God just wiped out the whole lot of them.

I couldn't understand the ending. I mean, why couldn't Moses get into the Promised Land? I asked my Father and He said search him, the ways of the Lord are inscrutable, but Marian said she bet it was because being a messenger of God, Moses already had his reward.

He said, "You know, it's not my favorite subject, and I'm no authority, but I think you might very well be right."

It's beyond me. I liked watching Pharaoh and the pyramids and Egypt and all that, but my favorite part is still about the golden idol, because it proved that there *was* a God and He didn't tolerate any messing around. (At least not with the Israelites. Or does it prove anything?)

If only I were an Israelite I'd know for sure. I am so awfully tired of praying and getting absolutely nowhere, even though I keep reading over that thing on charity where it says, "Though I have all faith, so that I could remove mountains . . ."

It's all very well *saying* it, but where do you *get* faith?

If there was only some way I could test it, to find out for sure if *there is* a God, and if so, if He is only for the Israelites.

Ann Landers says everybody should make a will, so having nothing better to do this afternoon, which is raining cats and dogs, I will.

First I shall list my valuables. Later I will have to decide who is to have what.

As I open the sloping desk lid, I really don't know where to begin.

My treasures are wrapped in tissue paper and, for me, neatly stored. Marian is very neat by nature, but I'm kind of a slob, except for my valuables.

First there is the napkin on which Mr. Romanov wrote.

There is a tiny gold ring with a diamond chip in it that won't even fit on my little finger that Bud gave me when he went away. He gave Marian one, too.

There is a pansy that the real Ann Carleon pressed in the family Bible when she was ten. It is like mauve parchment and I rarely unwrap it because I am afraid it will crumble.

There are four beautiful marbles that I found in a jam jar in the basement. One is so beautiful I don't think I would change it for the Polar Star.

There is Palgrave's *Golden Treasury of Verse*, which Miss Swanson gave me.

There are all my bubble-gum series cards, which I have outgrown, so just for the hell of it I think I'll leave them to Marian.

There are my six dirty pictures, which I found outside the sex theater downtown last fall.

There are three plaster casts of our right hands, which we all made in kindergarten at different times.

There is a solid-gold, old-fashioned fountain pen with a little kind of lever to let the ink into a rubber bladder only there isn't any bladder. It used to be His and since it doesn't work He said I could have it.

There is my embroidery, every stitch a tear in the night, forever unfinished.

There are the two wisdom teeth I had pulled last year. I think I'll have them made into pendant earrings when I have my ears pierced.

Then there are three huge English pennies with Queen Victoria's picture on them, and my Japanese fan with the fake ivory handle carved like lace, but the paper is all so broken and torn that I don't know whether it's worth listing.

Oh, yes. There are some newspaper clippings and pictures from the sports page of Conn O'Rourke.

Then there is the most valuable thing of all.

The May Spoon.

This is as good a time as any to explain about the May

Spoon. I've put it off because I really didn't know how. I mean, how do you describe something that is extremely valuable and yet is just an old bent spoon? The nearest thing I can think of is the Stone of Scone we read about in English History, which is just an old stone that sits under the Queen's throne and has been there for hundreds of years.

Like the Stone of Scone, the May Spoon is shrouded in mystery and has magic qualities. It is a very, very old spoon. No one knows how old. Either Marian or I found it in the garden when I was four years old. We both said it was called the May Spoon, but we didn't know why. It wasn't May when we found it. We both claimed to have found it but personally I believe I did.

Anyway, we fought over it so much and for so long and neither of us would eat off anything else but the May Spoon that Mumma finally hid it. I found it at the back of the silver drawer in the buffet last year.

Marian just laughed and said it wasn't magic at all and I could have it for all she cared. She is making a big mistake. There is really something very strange about it.

I can remember the sky that afternoon. We were in the back garden, eating raspberries off the bushes. It must have been late summer.

Mumma had given each of us a little shovel, the ones we used to take to the beach, and we were digging. I remember the smell of the afternoon, sniffing the green tomatoes and the raspberries and wallflowers and the grass, which had just been cut. Everything smelled very distinct and different.

But the oddest thing was the sky. Suddenly it was all curious colors. Marian says now it was just a rainbow, *but I don't think so*.

There was something odd and unusual about everything that afternoon. Marian knows—we both know—that there was something odd about the whole thing but I suppose we'll never know just what.

Today my word is hopefully. To be correct I should say that today my word is not hopefully. You Know Who grinds His teeth every time He hears Marian or me say hopefully. There is such a word but, He says, it is invariably used wrongly. There ought to be, he says, the word hopeably, which means what we are trying to convey. But since there isn't a hopeably, it is correct for me to say I hope, or one can hope or one would hope. But no hopefully.

So He said, "As a matter of fact, I'll invent the word, just for you."

As I've heard him say, words are cheap. He very generously gave me the new word, a word, He says, that is all mine. Brand new and never used. Hopeably. My very own word. Hopeably. Huh.

Go forth, He said, and spread the word. Let it be your Gospel. Hopeably, he says, I may stamp out a repellent lapsus linguae, whatever that is.

Gird your loins, He said, and go down in history as the girl who, alone and unafraid, stamped out hopefully.

So off I go. I'd like to be famous for *something*.

Yesterday as I was about to enter the Mall I saw Mrs. Lamb. She was way off from the building, in the parking lot. It was raining torrents and she stood there holding an umbrella with one hand and her pamphlets with the other. I quickly dropped my eyes to her feet. She was wearing old, cracked black oxfords, lumpy where somebody else's bunions had once been.

She recognized me and started to speak, "Isabel, my dear—"

And then I did the most terrible thing I have ever done. I walked right past her and into the Mall as if I were blind and deaf.

It haunts me. I know I was wrong to do it, but there's something *wrong* with the whole setup. There's something wrong about their religion, their joy, and their being so sure they will be saved.

I have to be honest and say it's more than that. I just can't stand poor old Mr. Lamb having no legs. It gives me the creeps and that's the truth of it. And I don't want to believe in a world where everybody has to be blown up just to save a few people, and I also don't think that's what Jesus had in mind.

But nevertheless, I don't know when I have felt so awful. Of all the lousy things I have ever done, this is the worst. Mrs. Lamb is good and nice, and so is he. It's just that their beliefs, their home, their lives, and even their bodies are ugly, ugly, ugly. And I don't want to see it.

Last night I cried myself to sleep thinking about poor old Mrs. Lamb standing out there in the rain and it was no good telling myself she didn't *have* to, or maybe she's right and she's going to heaven and I'm not.

I feel bad and I feel guilty. Bonnie is right, I am the limit.

Thus conscience does make cowards of us all. Miss Swanson once said that in Shakespeare's day conscience really meant consciousness but in my case it all adds up to the same thing.

Oh, hell!

After staying awake half the night being conscious of Mrs. Lamb I went over to the Colonel's for a game of billiards after school.

151

Carruthers is getting to be a real pain in the butt, security being very tight, and just to top everything off, the Colonel was in one of his foul moods.

I had spent most of my school day yawning and dozing, but once I got to the Colonel's I woke up and beat the pants off him at billiards. He sulked like a four year old.

He sat fuming in front of the billiard-room fire with his scotch and soda in his hand muttering, "The devil take them! The devil take the lot of them!"

I sat nursing my ginger beer and feeling bad about Mrs. Lamb.

"Did you ever do something awful, really awful and yet if you were given another chance you know you would probably do the same thing again?" I asked.

He twiddled the fingers of his left hand on the arm of his chair, twitched his mustache, and then he turned his pale, old blue, bloodshot eyes to me.

"Never look back, girl. Never look back. If you do, the past will creep up in the dark behind you and—" Here he ran his finger across his throat and said "Aarrghhh."

"Get me another peg," he said, holding out his glass. Sometimes I think he thinks I am his butler.

"The Devil take them!" he whispered again as I handed him his drink. "*He* thinks he'll catch me off guard, but he won't."

He sat staring into the flames. After a long while he suddenly turned to me.

"I once concocted, no, I'd say invented, a miraculous salve for horses. Then I found it worked for people, too. It worked on rheumatism, sprains, arthritis, and neuritis. It contained secret ingredients: eastern plants, western stabilizers, oil of hashish. Well, not exactly; it was really an arcana of hemp. I could have patented it and been a multimillionaire like Guinness or Colman. You know what Colman said about his mustard? It's not what they eat, it's what they leave on their plates."

"Why didn't you?" I asked.

He didn't answer for so long I was beginning to think he hadn't heard me, then, again suddenly, he turned and said, "Me in trade? I am a soldier, my dear McMurry. Mammon has never been my idol. Besides, what would be the use? Carruthers would only have blackmailed me for more. Oh! idol worshipers, all of them! Damned iconophiles! And Carruthers the worst of the lot!"

"The Devil take him!" he shouted.

"Is there really a Devil?" I asked.

His reply was very modern, for the Colonel.

"You'd better believe it," he said. Then he seemed to tire of the subject. "Fill the dog's water dish on your way out. And secure the gate firmly. I shall be around to check it out later."

I have an idea. It came to me last night, almost like a revelation. I guess it had to do with the Colonel's talk about idols. My idea is so simple that I don't know how I didn't think of it before. I feel kind of scared, and I'm not quite sure how to go about it, but the plan is so very, very simple.

I shall build an idol and I shall worship it.

God will *have* to do something to prove He exists if I worship an idol. That is, of course, if He does exist.

I admit it's sort of risky. I mean, I'm not even fourteen yet and it wouldn't be fair to go around striking kids dead even if you are God, but that doesn't mean He wouldn't do it. There were probably kids among the Israelites when they built their golden calf. Of course, *I* won't be able to afford gold.

I am a bit scared. I wish I knew more about building idols. It's not the sort of thing you can ask your family about or look up in the library.

It makes me want to laugh, if making idols and flirting with death is anything to laugh about.

"Pardon me, Miss Sinclair, but I'd like to make an idol. Under what section would I find idol-making?"

Do-it-yourself? Carpentry? Sculpture? Religion? Home Improvement?

Or maybe Gold-Plating, How to, Calves and Cows.

If I know Miss Sinclair she wouldn't bat an eye and would just say "Look it up in the index, under idols, please. It will be cross-filed."

The whole idea is sort of mind-boggling. I admit I'm a little leary, but—nothing ventured, nothing gained, as He says.

When I got home from school yesterday I did what I always do. I threw my schoolbooks on the kitchen table and yelled "Hi, everybody!" Then I went out on the back porch to bring in Peggy and have some cinnamon toast before taking her for our walk.

I went out on the back porch as usual, but Peggy wasn't there. I called her, but she didn't come. I got the dog whistle, which hangs on the back porch, and which only a dog can hear. I blew it for her, but she still didn't come. When I went back into the kitchen He came in with Mumma. I decided to have some cookies instead of toast but the cookie jar was empty. Fatso had beaten me to it.

"There aren't any cookies," I said. "Where's Peggy?"

They just stood there and looked at me.

"What's the matter?" I said. I suddenly knew something was wrong. For a minute I thought maybe something had happened to Marian and I felt sort of sick but she came in from the dining room eating a cookie and crying.

Everything was very quiet.

Then I said again, "Where's Peggy?"

They all looked at each other.

"She's gone away," He said finally.

"I don't understand. Where did she go?"

"She's gone to the vet's."

"Why? Is she sick? What's the matter with her?"

Nobody said anything again.

"Why, Why?" I asked. I began to feel panicky. "Why?"

"It was the only thing that could be done," He said.

"I don't understand what you mean," I said.

"They put her to sleep," said Marian.

I sat at the table. I began to cry.

Nobody said a word.

So I said, "Why did you do it? It's not right! It's not right!"

"It was the only humane thing to do," He said. "She was crippled and she had cancer. She would have suffered. You wouldn't want her to suffer, would you?"

Why, when people do something rotten, do they always put the blame on you?

"You killed her!" I shouted. "You killed Peggy!"

He didn't say a word. He just turned around and walked out of the room. He didn't even say he was sorry or anything.

I went up to my room and cried and cried and cried.

Peggy was older than me. I can't remember a time without her. She was half liver-colored pointer and half collie and was sort of funny-looking, but she was the smartest dog I ever knew. She understood everything I said to her. Sometimes I used to think she could read my mind.

Tonight at dinner I was so upset I almost said it. I know someday I will. The only thing that stops me is maybe it wouldn't be the right thing, but I'm getting surer and surer.

After dinner I took Bud's plate from the table like I always do and went to the back porch to scrape the scraps into Peggy's dish.

There was no Peggy's dish.

I sat down and began to cry and went to put my arm around Peggy's neck.

There was no Peggy.

First no beach and now no Peggy and even if there were a beach there wouldn't be a Peggy and if there were a Peggy there wouldn't be a beach. No Peggy, no beach, no mountains, no Miss Swanson, no Bonnie.

I can't stand much more of this.

It's been five days since I have written in my diary. I am mourning Peggy and I couldn't think of any other way to do it. Words can never express the ache I feel.

Well, I've had a brainwave in the meanwhile. Sometimes it wouldn't surprise me to learn that I have a touch of genius.

I was lying in bed thinking about my idol when it struck me like a bolt of lightning: I have one right in the house, in the box-room cupboard, behind the Christmas decorations.

What could be better? A sheep is as good as a calf. And even if it isn't golden, I can do all sorts of things to make it idolatrized. The possibilities are endless.

First I need a base to put it on.

There are some leftover bricks piled against the garage from the chimney repair and they will be perfect. I will build shoulders in a little platform, and then a neck and then put the skull on that. I'll put it in the front of the closet so I'll have light when the door is open.

I can't wait to begin. It was ages before I could get to sleep, I was so excited.

This morning when I woke up I stared at the real Anne for a long time. I wish she was here so we could talk about it. I'll bet she would have some neat ideas.

I've got the platform of the shoulders and neck built for my idol. It took me longer than I thought because I had to sneak the bricks up two at a time under my coat and be sure no one was around.

It looks sturdy but kind of clumsy and amateurish.

I also got the skull out today and it's absolutely perfect, so much so that you hardly notice the shoulders and neck. Boy, what an Idol. You wouldn't believe how gruesome the teeth are.

I miss Peggy so much it hurts. I just can't believe she's not here. Where is she now? I don't mean her body.

They took her to the pound and they burn dead dogs there. I mean, was she like people are supposed to be and did she have a soul? I really can't believe she didn't if we have. She was so old and wise and gentle that I can't believe she lived sixteen years for *nothing*.

He said we could get another dog but I don't want one.

The dogs around here are all crazy. There is a corgi up the

block who is so flaky you wouldn't believe it. Next door to the corgi lives an insane German shepherd called Buster. Buster was standing minding his own business for once, with his mouth open and his tongue hanging out. Taffy, the corgi, ran up to him, put his dumb head right in Buster's mouth and bit his tongue. Needless to say, Buster's crocodile teeth crunched down on Taffy's face and it cost two hundred dollars at the vet's to have it sewn back on. The people who own Buster have to go to the post office for their mail because the postman won't go in their yard.

The real character, though, and a good friend of mine is Beau, the village murderer. He's a huge English pit bulldog, as gentle as a lamb with people, but dogs, watch out! Beau has a barrel chest, twinkling, sly little shoe-button eyes, huge cheekbones, and jaws like a hyena.

Even Buster, when he sees those tattered pointed ears whizzing around a corner, pretends he's not interested and hurries off to hide in his doghouse.

A couple of streets away there is a Great Dane who has heart trouble. Once he lies down he is so gawky he has trouble getting up again. He is always lying down in the middle of the road and he is going to get run over one of these days.

And the poodles! West Van seems to be infested with them, in all sizes and colors. If you put a bounty on them like they do on coyotes, you could make a fortune. Some wear little bows, jeweled collars and nail polish on their toenails. I even saw one, on a windy day on Dundarave pier, who had on a little fur jacket.

There are a lot of rare dogs here, little fuzzy Tibetan things, and huge Hungarian dogs with coats that look like they just been permanented. There are Basenjis and Afghans and Aleuts and English pugs. Debbie Cunningham has an English pug they have had for years and it has managed to bite every single member of the family. Jill St. Lawrence has a purebred cocker spaniel that is retarded. I'm not trying to be funny. It really is. It has never been housebroken and still doesn't know its own name.

I don't want a fancy dog, and I certainly don't want a dog like any of those. I want a dog like Peggy. As a matter of fact, I just want Peggy.

Oh joy! Oh happiness!

He is going to Europe for three weeks! I'm so happy I'm ready to turn somersaults. And to think I wrote that nothing decent ever happens around here.

There's a great bustle, with Marian having to get his evening clothes pressed, and passports and visas and the phone ringing off the hook. He is actually going to be gone three whole weeks. Boy, are the mice going to play around here.

Well, he finally got off, in a rotten mood, swearing and losing his temper over things like his shirt studs and the keys to his luggage. Marian said she felt like putting the damn things on a string and hanging them around his neck. (She didn't say that to him, of course.) She drove him to the airport.

I phoned Bonnie right away. She said, "Yeah, that's good news. I read about him in the newspaper."

I waited for her to ask me over. She's married now, and lives with her policeman in West Vancouver only about ten blocks from us. I haven't seen her since she got married. I have missed her very much, almost as much as Peggy. I have phoned her a lot of times but she said she was expecting a baby and was very busy and would phone me when she felt up to it. As a matter of fact it's been months since I have seen her. I was sort of hurt she didn't phone me, but, as she used to say, that's life for you.

Finally she said, "If you can square it with Marian, come for dinner tomorrow. You can walk over and Bernie will drive you home."

I was very happy and forgave her.

I told Marian, who He told to look after me, that a friend had invited me to dinner and I would be home by ten.

She said, "Listen, stupido, I know you're going to Bonnie's. You don't have to be a genius to figure that out."

It's her rotten way of saying I have no friends.

"Well, go if you want. You and I can be a lot of use to each other if we play it right. Of course I'm not going to tell Him, which is the next question you'll ask. But if I decide to ask you for a favor later on, then you've got to help me."

I promised.

I wore my best dress, the black taffeta, but I didn't wear Mumma's combs or the cameo.

They live on the fifth floor of a nice apartment and have a view of the water. I got there early.

I could hardly believe my eyes when I saw Bonnie. She is absolutely huge with child. I can't understand it. She has only been married three months.

She asked where I got the dress. I told her, and then asked her if she liked it.

She said it looked very expensive.

He stood up when I entered the living room. I had made up my mind I wouldn't like him, but that I wouldn't show it. But he's really neat. He's a great big guy. The top of my head comes to the middle of his chest. He didn't talk down to me or treat me like a kid. Bonnie and Bernie, I think that's really neat.

We had fried chicken and potato salad and ice cream and chocolate cake for dinner. I ate till I thought I'd bust.

"Well, I must say your appetite has sure improved," Bonnie said. "I'm surprised you haven't put on any weight."

She turned to him. "She used to be the pickiest damn kid in the world. She didn't like *anything*. I've always been amazed she didn't drop dead from malnutrition."

He laughed but I didn't think it was very funny.

She seemed different, more like other grown-ups. I suppose it's because she's going to have a baby. She didn't talk very much but she did say if the baby is a girl they would call it Ann after me.

After dinner Bernie and I did kung fu and I won. It was loads of fun but Bonnie got sort of mad about the noise and said, "For God's sake, Bernie, grow up! We just got in this place. Do you want us thrown out?"

He sounded like a ton of bricks every time I threw him.

He said, "Okay, honey," and when her back was turned he winked at me and said how about some TV. We turned to a series about policemen in Los Angeles and she said, "God, Bernie! If I see one more of those dumb cop shows I'll scream! Can't you get something over the seven-year age level?"

He said, "Okay, okay, honey," and turned on one of those cultural programs—called *The Ascent of Man.*

"*Oh, honestly!*" This time she almost shouted. "Isn't there any halfway measure with you? Who wants to watch that stuff?"

Then he said how about us having a game of Scrabble, so we did. He was pretty good for a policeman. I always thought they were kind of dumb with words, but he beat me.

At nine-thirty Bonnie said she thought I ought to go because of school tomorrow.

Bonnie has sold her old car but he's got one nearly as old. On the way home he said,

"You mustn't be upset if Bonnie acts sort of irritated. Women get that way when they're expecting their first babies and she hasn't been feeling too good. Her legs bother her a lot and the doctor says she's got to keep off her feet. And she hated losing her figure. She gets bored just sitting around the apartment all the time. I wish you could visit us more often. You really cheer her up, and she talks about you all the time. Of course, I appreciate the difficulties regarding your father."

I said I understood how Bonnie felt and I was sorry. He'll never know how sorry. She seemed like somebody else.

"Things will be different once the baby's born," he said. "Then, if your parents don't object, you can come up and visit us anytime."

I guess he was trying to tell me in as nice a way as possible that she wouldn't be asking me back for a while.

I thought I might cry, so I got out of the car quickly.

"Thank you for tonight," I said. "I really enjoyed myself."

"So did I," he said. I believed him.

He looked so big and kind that I took my courage in both hands and said, "I like you a lot, Bernie. If Bonnie had to marry someone, I'm glad it was you."

He looked embarrassed and said, "I like you, too, Isabel. I'm sorry tonight wasn't more of a success. Keep your chin up."

And he drove off.

I went up to my room and cried.

I understand how prisoners feel. All the time they are in jail they think everything will be perfect if they could just get out. But it isn't.

162

Once I read a poem that said something about how you can ruin everything just by being there.

Well, that's me. I wish I knew who wrote it. I would write him a letter, except that with our luck it would get lost in the mail.

Yesterday I had a good game with the Colonel. For a change I won. I guess you would say I couldn't help but win, as I finally got to be Wellington instead of Napoleon in the battle of Waterloo. Also, the Colonel's getting to be a better sport and doesn't cheat so much, so I don't either.

There are hardly any battles we haven't played, and he's given me some interesting books to read, which You Know who immediately grabbed.

Yes, He's back. So far He's behaving Himself rather nicely. I think He might actually have missed us. He brought us both back handmade Swedish silver necklaces and bracelets.

He is still dying to play with the Colonel but it's no dice. Carruthers is a real pain in the ass now, if you'll pardon the expression.

But it's really fun to get all your armies laid out on the billiard table. The Colonel says his collection of toy soldiers is the best in North America and he is going to leave them to the British War Museum in his will. They are worth more than half a million dollars, but he says they are priceless. Most are from the eighteenth and nineteenth centuries, but like I said before, some are very ancient, like the Chinese black jade ones. We have to wear cotton gloves when we play with any of them because sweat can damage their finishes.

And it still doesn't matter how much He nags to be allowed over to the Colonel's. The Colonel still says no.

No men is the rule. They might be Carruthers in disguise. The Colonel says Carruthers is getting increasingly cunning.

The Colonel is very polite about not seeing my "Pater" as he calls him, and always sends his regrets that he is unable to receive company due to ill health.

When I went for a walk on the beach yesterday, Primo called me back.

"Where's you dog?" he asked.

One of the men, Salvatore, used to give Peggy pieces of Italian sausage from his lunch. He had a piece of sausage in his hand now.

We stood looking at each other. He doesn't speak English. I wanted to speak directly to him but I didn't know how.

Finally I shrugged my shoulders and pointed my finger straight up to the sky.

I could tell by his eyes he understood right away.

I turned and walked off. I heard him say something to Primo. Primo called me back.

"He say he is sorry."

I do have a friend. Wouldn't you know he can't speak English.

I played at the Colonel's yesterday, and he was in a horrible mood. He was sure Carruthers had been prowling around the night before. During the battle of Balaclava he swept all my men over with his cane and said,

"Oh, God! If only I could get my hands on him!"

I got up and put all the soldiers back in their positions. Then I said, "I'm not playing with you any more today."

We glared at each other and he smashed his cane against the table so hard all the soldiers fell down again. I just got up and left.

Today he was waiting at his gate for me. He didn't apologize but said would I join him for a dish of chocolate ice cream, which he knows I love. I went in, not for the ice cream, but because I really felt sorry for him. When we were setting up the soldiers for Culloden he mumbled that Carruthers was driving him mad and that he really wasn't himself yesterday.

I said I understood but he said no, I didn't. I couldn't.

"It's the nights, the nights!" he cried.

I said he really didn't have to worry because we both knew Rommel would tear anyone to pieces who came prowling around.

"Not Carruthers," he whispered. "He can't get his teeth in Carruthers. I don't know what I am going to do."

"I'm sorry," I said. "But I really don't think my father would let me sleep overnight."

He nodded and said, "Yes, I must pull myself together. After all, I am a soldier. You see, my dear McMurry, that's what Carruthers wants to do. He wants to destroy my integrity. That's what he was always after. And what better way to destroy a soldier's integrity than to make a coward out of him?"

Boring day. My word is exaggerate. I only have to remember how to spell it. I already know what it means.

Today in English class, while everybody else was thinking of clausal analysis, I was thinking of my idol. If you've got an idol, you've got to have an altar.

I did go to the library, and the books were actually under

idols! I also got out books on ancient and primitive religions and the books say the idols always have altars. You see, you need them for your sacrifices.

Now, I ask you, how do you go about getting an altar? There are no pictures of them in the books and none in our encyclopedia and I'm afraid to ask too many questions either at home or at the library.

Well, just when Elise Woodsley had to go up to the board and parse a sentence, it came to me. I will never think of my altar without thinking of Elise Woodsley, even in my old age, so in a way, my idol has made Elise Woodsley immortal.

We have, at the back of the box-room closet, among the junk, an East Indian table, with folding legs of carved wood about ten inches high, and the top is a huge brass tray that fits onto it. He bought it at one of his auctions and it turned out to have been made in Bangladesh, and wasn't old at all. He got so mad he threw it at the back of the box-room closet.

It was made for the job.

Not much to report on the home front except that my idol is coming along splendidly. I have painted red lips around his amber teeth and it makes him look really quite awful.

Among the Christmas decorations I found two gold balls. They fit perfectly into his ear holes. Behind each of them I have put a small bunch of artificial red geraniums that stick up about four inches, like fiery little antennas.

In the junk at the back of the closet I also found a pair of white baby boots, probably mine or Marian's. Anyway, I put one on each side of the shoulders, just slightly in front and painted red toenails on them. They look like real ugly little feet.

I have collected all the junk jewelry in the house and also got some from Bonnie. I phoned her up and she gave me quite a lot. I think her conscience bothers her about not bothering to give me a bit of her time. When I went to pick them up she started talking about her varicose veins. I said I was in a hurry. I also told her I wanted the jewelry for dressing up. She really thinks I am so childish I am still doing that on rainy afternoons. People will believe anything.

My idol's neck is now festooned with paste pearls, diamonds, and rubies, his ears and brow are adorned with every color stone you can think of. With his scarlet lips and golden ears he is becoming more fearsome and godlike every day.

Well, I'm still in a quandary. The books on idolatry say you got to have a sacrifice on your altar.

Where am I going to get a sacrifice? It seems a pity to have got this far and then to be stumped by some dumb sacrifice. I just get over one hurdle and there's another in front of me.

I'll just have to wait and see what I can come up with. People's minds, I'm beginning to suspect, are much more inventive than they realize.

My Father keeps saying He would give his right arm just to *see* those soldiers and that I don't know how lucky I am.

The Colonel tried teaching me chess but I was slow learning, which irritated him so much he gave up. I guess we're stuck with battles, canasta, Scrabble, (I'm a whiz at that so naturally the Colonel doesn't care too much for it), dominoes, and backgammon.

The Colonel is like a kid about games. He is really crazy about them. He's *got* to win and sulks when he doesn't, but I don't let him get away with it. If he cheats, I cheat. If he sulks, I sulk. If he throws things around too much, I do, too, and I tell him if he doesn't like it he can find somebody else to play with, which works because he can't find anybody else to trust about Carruthers.

The Colonel says he is afraid they will lock him up if they find out about Carruthers. When I asked where they would lock him up he got real mean and said I was trying to pry secret information out of him and all he was required to tell me was name, rank, and serial number. I got kind of bored at that point and said I was going home.

When I got to the front gate he came running up, gasping and panting, "You will come back, you will come back, won't you?"

I get fed up with him and I was mad so I was cruel and said, "Only if you say please."

It just about killed him, but he did.

Well, I've done it. I always knew I would someday, and I always knew it had to be done. I didn't really want to do it but I had to.

At dinner last night she said,

"Baby dear, you haven't set Buddy's place. Hurry, dear, he'll be here soon."

I took a deep breath and then I said very slowly that Bud would not be here.

He looked at me and a vein started throbbing in His forehead. Marian's face went very white.

It was as if I were a ventriloquist's dummy and somebody was speaking through me.

"Bud won't be here for dinner tonight. Or tomorrow night or the night after. He will never be here. Bud is dead."

His fists were clasping and unclasping. Marian's eyes were sort of glassy.

My mother looked at me and shook her head. Then she said,

"Child, you don't know what you are saying."

"Bud is dead," I said again.

He crumpled his napkin and said in a very soft voice, "Leave this table."

I left. I felt as though a million pounds had been taken off my shoulders. I went to my room and looked up at the real Anne.

"It was all a lie," I told her. "Someone had to tell the truth. Somebody should have years ago."

I felt very tired and fell asleep with my clothes on and didn't wake up till morning. I didn't dream anything.

Nothing happened today either. I thought maybe God would strike me dead, that is, of course, if there is one. Well, we'll soon know, won't we?

My mother *does* look strangely different, in just a little way. She sat with a very thoughtful expression on her face for a long while after dinner tonight, staring at me.

When she spoke to me she called me Marian and said how terribly quickly I had grown. Marian looked at Him and then at me. All of us were puzzled and a little bit afraid.

But a second later she was back at her needlework, happily smiling and humming.

I have thought and thought and thought about the sacrifice now that I have my altar, and I am getting nowhere.

My father and mother and sister are obviously out of the question and if Peggy were alive, that would be even more unthinkable.

The book on Micronesian Islanders says they cut off one of their fingers or toes to placate their gods but I think that's going too far. After all, this *is* just an idol, and an experiment to boot, and with my luck there wouldn't be any God and I'd have whacked off a finger for nothing.

Besides, I can't stand blood, my own in particular.

I thought of a name for my Idol last night. I am going to call it Gog, the heathen god who comes out of Russia.

It would be awful to have to give up now, when things are going so perfectly. I put two red Christmas candles inside Gog's skull, behind the eyeholes, and decorated his body with gold and silver Christmas tinsel ropes, and with the jewelry, the golden ball ears and the red flowers behind them, you just have to see Gog to describe the effect.

You honestly wouldn't believe just how idolized this collection of stuff I have put together seems. When the candle flames tremble in Gog's skull the eyeholes look like liquid rubies, the orbs of a real demon-god. Gog glistens and shimmers and sparkles all over with his pagan jewels and in the flickering shadows he seems alive.

That son of a bitch of a Beatrice came up to me in the hall after English yesterday. There were about four Camorras, wearing their new jackets with their insignias on the pockets, all standing around, plus five or six other kids.

Beatrice said, "Say, Isabel, we've changed the rules. We're taking in more members. If you'd like to join again we'll sign you in."

I looked at her.

I said, "Piss off."

Then I walked away.

I'm not sorry I said it. I'm just sorry I joined the mob.

Later, in the washroom, Naomi Schinbein came up to me.

"Why don't you join again, Isabel?"

I have been thinking a lot about what Marian said about offering condolences, so, although, like the Colonel, it just about killed me, I did. I said,

"I'm sorry about your brother. I'm sorry I didn't say I was sorry sooner."

She just nodded and said, "Thank you," and began to walk away, but then she stopped and came back.

"Well, why *don't* you join again?"

Now how can you explain something like that? So I just said, "I'm not joining because I don't want to."

"You know why she asked you, don't you? It's because your father won that award and got his picture in the paper. I'll bet her father put her up to it. They're awful snobs."

"So am I," I said. "That's why I won't join your rotten club."

It really was terrible of me to say that, but I have to admit I enjoyed it.

"Well, gee! Don't get mad at me!" Naomi said. "It wasn't my idea getting you out of the club. As a matter of fact I voted for you to stay."

"Well, it didn't do either of us any good, did it?"

I had no idea until then how really bitter I felt about it. I don't know when I've been so just plain mean.

"I tried," said Naomi. "It wasn't easy. I mean, particularly for me. It isn't easy to go against a crowd."

Then she said something I didn't understand.

"That's Yiddish," she said. "I don't speak it but my father says that all the time. It means it's difficult to be a Jew."

Yeah? Well she ought to try being Irish around our house for a week or so.

I don't know what made me say it, but I said, "Well, *my* Father says, 'And in the night Balthazar was murdered by his slaves.' "

She blinked.

"What's that supposed to mean?"

I didn't know either so I said, "If the shoe fits, wear it."

"I simply don't understand you," she said. "I was only trying to be friendly."

Well, I could have told her right then and there that nobody could be friendly with that snake in the grass and me at the same time. Instead, I said,

"You're too late. You should have done something more than just vote against Beatrice. You should have spoken up then, like you are now."

Me, the world's biggest coward, was talking. I ought to be ashamed of myself. Why don't I pick on that rotten Beatrice?

Naomi only shrugged. "Well, if that's the way you want it, go ahead. Cut off your nose to spite your face."

Even then I couldn't let her have the last word.

"Remember what I said, and warn Beatrice," I said. " 'In the night Balthazar was murdered by his slaves.' And my Father says it was written by a Jew."

What that had to do with this crazy conversation, I don't know, except that it sounded ominous and I hoped it would get back to Beatrice.

Ominous is a very good, strong word, which I learned about three weeks ago.

Naomi just shrugged in a bored way and walked off, which was what *I* was intending to do.

Mrs. Lamb no longer stands around the parking lot at Park Royal. I asked the uniformed man about her. He said she was asked not to come back as people complained of being harassed. I can't imagine poor Mrs. Lamb harassing anybody.

When I was wandering around the Mall, the most super thing happened. You remember Jane Lonsdale, who was engaged to Fraser Schinbein and who played with the Ouija board? Well, I met her and she asked me, believe it or not, to have tea with her in the *Bon Gourmet*! Although I have walked past the Bon Gourmet many, many times, I have never been in there, and what is more I never expected to go in there. I had only a bit of money left from Aunt Ada's last letter, so of course it was out of the question and I had to explain to Jane that unfortunately I was temporarily out of funds. She laughed and said she had expected to be my host when she asked me.

We went in and I was very nervous. As a matter of fact, I shook. It is a very posh place and I started reading this huge menu about the size of a newspaper and I couldn't understand most of it. Jane said how about a selection of French pastries and I said I thought that would be particularly adequate. The waiter brought this silver dish and Jane said just point to the one you want so I did and he put it on my plate with silver tongs.

Jane said, oh, that's not enough, Isabel, take two more, so I did, then she said I must also take one for her as she was dieting and I would be doing her a favor, so I did.

They were absolutely gorgeous and looked like pictures from a book, all shiny with glazed fruits on top and many-colored icings, some with layers of custards and whipped cream under them and each looking like a little bouquet.

Jane said her idea of heaven when she was my age was to sit and eat French pastries until eternity. I also had coffee, which I ordered because she did and we never have it at home. (He says his money is not going to support those bastards, whoever they are.) To tell you the truth I really don't like coffee very much but it wasn't too bad with the pastries. Jane had a small carafe of white wine and a watercress sandwich.

We talked and talked and talked. She is very beautiful, with naturally blond hair that is so fair it looks phony and it isn't, and a complexion that is absolutely dazzling. Everyone is always remarking on what beautiful, fine skins Marian and I have, but I'm sure we look like mud fences next to Jane. She has rosy cheeks, and although her skin is as fair as ours, she gets this sort of biscuit-colored tan. She was born in England and has been back there many times. I told her about wanting to go to Haworth Parsonage and see the Brontë house, and I know you aren't going to believe this, but *she has been there!* Isn't that simply amazing? She says that although the country is bleak and forbidden it is extraordinarily beautiful.

She is going on a trip to Europe soon, before she starts her nursing training at the Vancouver General Hospital. I told her about my friend Anne Frank and she nodded and said she would go to her house in Amsterdam on my behalf.

Somehow the subject of Anne Frank got us to talking about Fraser Schinbein. I would never have dreamed of starting a conversation about him, as that would not be delicate, but she talked about him very openly.

She said she and Fraser never had any intention of getting married; as a matter of fact they didn't even like each other. They just said they did to bug their parents.

To tell you the truth I was a little shocked, but I am sure Jane couldn't do anything wrong.

His parents, when they heard about the marriage, said they would hold a ritual mourning for the dead for him.

Her parents, who she says are so monumentally dull they would make a cat laugh, couldn't come up with anything as brutal as that, having absolutely no imagination, but they told her, "If you marry that Jew we will never speak to you again."

Then she added, "And believe me, Isabel, they meant it."

I said I couldn't understand why people were born at all if they had to die as young as Fraser, and Jane said I must be thinking of my own brother.

I said yes and she said, well, you really couldn't compare the two. Fraser was doomed and it was only a matter of time, but Bud believed in something and died for his beliefs. His death had meaning and dignity, she said, while Fraser's sojourn on earth was some sort of cosmic slipup.

This got us on the subject of religion and I told her about my idol. She looked very peculiar, almost shocked for a minute, then she said she had to give me a gold star for originality.

I explained about the Bible saying that God had destroyed the Israelites, and she said she certainly wouldn't like to think of me suffering the same fate.

I felt very brave and said there was nothing to be afraid of and there was no other way I could find out if there was a God to cure my mother.

She shook her head and said, "Well, I hope you know what you're doing. That's pretty heavy stuff you're into, Goldilocks."

I said I wished she was my sister instead of Marian, but she only shook her head again and said that when I was grown up I would find that Marian was the best friend I could ever have in this world. Then she said that in the meanwhile she sure wished she had a kid sister like me.

I really couldn't agree with her about Marian but she said just wait and see.

She seems to be right about everything else so maybe there's something in it.

I parted from her with great regret. Heaven only knows

when I will see her again. She said she would send me a postcard when she was away.

It was one of the most memorable days of my life and I shall always look back on it with the greatest happiness.

I am going to do a thing so terrible and awful that I hesitate to put pen to paper.

I have thought of a sacrifice for my altar, and it is a perfect one.

The sacrifice to be victimized on the Altar of Gog will be the Black Rose, Lady Clementine Churchill.

I really sincerely believe that if you ponder a problem sufficiently and bide your time, the answer will come to you.

I was just about ready to throw in the sponge about a sacrifice when, a couple of days ago, I was standing in the Colonel's garden petting Rommel and all of a sudden it hit me like a bolt of lightning.

I don't care what the Colonel says, it's a lot of baloney about plants feeling, so she is, actually, made for the job. She is also very rare and valuable, what the dictionary calls unique.

Yes, just one of a kind. There isn't another like her in the whole world and if that doesn't satisfy Gog, I don't know what would.

Wow! Beauty sacrificed on the Altar of the Beast Gog!

I can hardly wait.

In order to succeed in a venture such as I am about to embark on, as the Colonel would say, one must act with great circumspection before and with great imagination during its commission.

Well, that shouldn't be too hard. After all, I have been taught by a general and I have at my command that greatest of military advantages: surprise.

I lie awake every night now, going over each detail in my mind. It's like watching a movie. The more I think about it, the more automatic and easier it becomes. Get into the garden. Keep Rommel quiet. Force my way into the little greenhouse. Snatch the black rose from her quiet grave. Leave no clues behind. Make no noise.

Will it be best on a night of the full moon, or in the last quarter, with darkness as my ally?

My biggest worry—how not to leave footprints. The earth around the little greenhouse is freshly dug and when I was there yesterday I purposely walked on it and left very clear, deep footprints. The Colonel frowned, got a rake, and very carefully wiped them out, so I can't afford to leave more as his eye is on the sparrow where the Black Rose is concerned.

One by one, though, time is answering my problems. One by one they are being worked out. For instance, after disintering (a very fine word meaning taking out of the earth) Lady Clementine, I had been worried about leaving a trail of earth behind me like a paper chase, but I found a perfect-sized sack in our basement that will fill the bill as though it were ordered for the occasion. I'll just pop Lady Churchill, roots and all, right into it.

The key to the greenhouse has been a major worry to me, and I was reluctant to force the lock because of the noise. TV solved that problem. All you have to do is tape one of the glass squares, break it, then cut through the wooden side of the door to which the lock is secured. I am always amazed at what you can learn watching television.

I was quite jubilant about this solution, when lo and behold,

I have been wasting my valuable time. Yesterday I visited the Colonel and I saw him put the key away. You simply wouldn't believe where he put it.

It's under a rock about ten feet from the greenhouse. Granted there are ornamental rocks everywhere in the garden, and I suppose nobody would turn them all over on the off chance somebody might be dumb enough to hide a key there, but from a military viewpoint, it's a bust.

The footprints are still a problem. There is no way I can approach the greenhouse from any side without leaving marks on the freshly dug-up ground, which the Colonel rakes daily to keep smooth.

Of course. The old fox. It only occurred to me now that this is a deliberate military strategy of the Colonel's so that no one can approach without leaving a sign. I should have known, as he would say, my enemy's defenses.

I have finally decided to carry a rake and cover my footprints as I back up. It's going to really complicate things as our rake is six feet long and heavy and I already have to take along a spade to dig up Lady Clementine. Then, of course, as I am leaving, I will also have Lady Clementine to carry and I have no idea how much she weighs. I don't know if I can manage the whole works. I will just have to keep thinking.

Also, I have decided not to go out on the night of the full moon. Marian says it has been proven statistically that people are nuttier than usual at that time and the Colonel is nutty enough at the best of times. It would be very easy, even if I carry a rake as well as the other things, to miss, and to leave behind just one fatal footprint. I shudder to think of the Colonel catching me, although I have to admit that the whole venture adds a bit of spice to my otherwise drab life.

Well, tonight is D-night and if would be folly to say that I am not without trepidation. That's my own word. I didn't have to look it up.

I have solved the problem of the footprints.

It's funny and just like I said before, if you think about a thing long enough, a solution always presents itself when you least expect it.

The solution came to me as I was brushing my teeth and feeling quite guilty about the way I treated Mrs. Lamb and Naomi Schinbein.

Since it is impossible to avoid approaching the greenhouse without leaving footprints, then, of course, I must leave footprints.

But not mine. I shall wear a pair of my Father's running shoes stuffed with Kleenex. There must be fifty million pairs of shoes just like them in West Vancouver and there is no way the Colonel can pin that one on me.

I wonder how soldiers feel about going into battle. I definitely have butterflies in my stomach. I don't know how the Colonel could have been so calm the way he says he always was.

Anyhow, there's only one approach: a job has to be done, and nobody can do it for me. Maybe that's the way real soldiers feel.

D-day is over. It went without a hitch. Rommel was delighted to see me and enjoyed the piece of meat I took him. I did not put blacking on my face like the commandos usually do because I thought it would be too much trouble to explain if my father caught me going out. Instead, after I left the house, I took a nylon stocking and wore it over my head with Marian's black tam on top of that. I wore a dark sweater and jeans and of course, my father's running shoes stuffed with Kleenex. At one point they nearly proved my undoing because I stepped right out of one of them and hung there in midair with my foot poised like a Balinese dancer until I managed to step back into it.

I wore heavy gloves because of the thorns. I am really amazed at my thoroughness.

It was difficult getting Lady Churchill out. I had no idea rosebushes had such long roots, but a few good tugs after digging around her bottom did the trick. I neatly shut and locked everything up, not forgetting to shake Rommel's paw and give him a kiss before I left, which was a mistake—he let out a tiny, high-pitched whine because he did not want me to go. Fortunately the Colonel has trained him to absolute silence by laying one forefinger on the tip of Rommel's snoot. If you do that, *nothing* could make him whine or bark.

Everyone was fast asleep when I got in and I sneaked up to the box room and hid Lady Clementine in the closet.

After removing my disguise I sat on my bed and looked up at the real Anne. I had intended to have a little chat with her, but the strangest thing happened.

My stomach had been in a knot before going into battle, but during the actual operation I had been too busy to feel much of anything. Now I didn't want to talk to Anne. I just lay back with my arms folded behind my head and stared at the ceiling, and I had this feeling of relaxation.

It was really a wonderful feeling. I have never experienced anything like it before and may never again.

I fell asleep with the light on and slept like a log until morning. Today I looked up all the words I could think of in the dictionary to describe how I felt.

Finally, in the entry for elation, I found what I was looking for: euphoria.

It was a mystical and May-Spoonish experience and euphoria is the word for it.

Idols have to be consecrated, which means have a ceremony to make them sacred. Yesterday I thought I'd have a dry run, sort of get everything ready for the real McCoy.

Lady Clementine lay across the brass tray. I lit the incense I had bought at Woolworths', and also the red Christmas candles in Gog's skull. He shimmered and glimmered, his big grey teeth grinned evilly.

The incense stank something awful. I closed the door behind me so it wouldn't seep through the house and lit an extra candle for light.

I stood staring at Gog's blazing eyes. I felt sort of rooted to the spot. Suddenly it seemed as if the flames behind his eyes crept out and hundreds of them began wheeling in space and up and down the walls.

Then, without warning, I felt sick to my stomach and sank to my knees. It was that pukey cheap incense. I knelt there wondering if I should go to the bathroom and try to throw up. The flames on the walls and in the air disappeared. Then, suddenly, there was the most frightful noise.

A tremendous bang that shook me from head to toe. I think I must have fainted for a few seconds, because the next thing I remember I was laying right out on the floor. It couldn't have been for very long, because the candles hadn't burnt down much.

I got up and blew them out and dropped the incense in a glass of water I had put there for that purpose, then I went out and closed the door.

At the foot of the stairs, in the front hall, I met Fatso. She looked at me and said, "What's the matter with you? You look awful. Did that explosion scare you?"

I heard thumping noises overhead.

"That's Daddy. He's up on the roof. He thought maybe the chimney fell over again."

A few minutes later He came in and said, "Well, whatever it was, it wasn't the chimney. It must have been a jet breaking the sound barrier right over the house. It's strange, they don't usually come this close to the mountains."

Later He phoned the police to ask. They said they had been besieged with calls from our block and they didn't know what it was either.

That was over twenty-four hours ago, and people are still trying to figure out what happened.

I am not going to tell them.

A letter today from Aunt Ada. It seemed particularly nice when we opened it because a ten-dollar bill fluttered out, but when we read the letter, it was fraught with tragedy.

The most awful things are happening back east. As if it isn't bad enough that Barney's becoming a priest! Father O'Shaughnessy will almost surely roast in hell forever.

Dietrich, who is a Communist, and who has been living in sin with another Communist, has decided to marry her. Aunt Ada says that the thought of his godless union was bad enough, but marriage is unbearable.

Uncle Billy, of course, is still drinking, gambling, and enjoying life.

Aunt Ada says she has turned the other cheek again and again, and to what avail, but though God punish her with scorpions, yet will she cherish Him.

"What does the part about scorpions mean?" I asked Marian. Even Marian didn't know, but she did say,

"You know what I *do* know? I know Aunt Ada is as nuts as everybody else in this family. Except me, of course."

Aunt Ada went on to say that she hoped one of her girls would come out to visit her this summer and Marian said that it sure as hell wasn't going to be her. I would kind of like to go just to get away from everything here, but I'm scared of going on a plane and traveling alone. I'm scared of going to a city I've never been in that is three times as large as Vancouver and twenty times as large as West Vancouver, and where everybody speaks French and hates Anglos, particularly Anglos who come from Britsh Columbia.

I'm also scared of Aunt Ada. Well, not like I'm scared of You Know Who, but I don't think I'd do so hot on this turning the mattress and scrubbing my nails bit. And I'd be just as lonely there as here because I wouldn't know *anybody*.

Marian says she really likes Aunt Ada, but better to suffer the slings and arrows of outrageous fortune here, which proves, if nothing else, that Shakespeare is really very handy.

No. I'd have to be really hard up to stay with Aunt Ada.

Aunt Ada wrote a whole page about our wicked Uncle Billy. Marian says he's really not *that* bad and that Aunt Ada's fixation about him shows impaired judgment. Since Aunt Ada also wrote half a page on how lucky we are to have such a wonderful father, I am inclined to agree with Marian.

Yesterday was consecration day for Gog.

Everything was ready. Lady Clementine lay across the brass tray in the lap of the idol. I lit the candles in Gog's skull and again everything shimmered and glimmered.

Gog looked radiantly glorious.

Then the downstairs phone rang.

Fatso called upstairs that it was for me.

I couldn't think who it could be, since nobody *ever* phones me. Well, I got downstairs and answered it and it was a lady who represents the "Ban The Leg Trap" group against inhumane methods of trapping animals. I had signed my name and address on a petition in the Park Royal Mall that was to be sent to Ottawa. This lady didn't know I was just a kid and wanted me to do some volunteer work. When she heard my voice she asked me how old I was and I told her. She said she was sorry but she didn't think I could do it unless I was older. I said good-bye and hung up and then I heard this unearthly shriek. It was like nothing you ever heard, a real high howl that trailed into a low howl.

My first thought was that something had happened to Peggy, but then I remembered there wasn't any Peggy anymore.

Then I knew what it was.

I closed my eyes while He went bounding up the stairs three at a time. I would gladly have spent the rest of my life on that two feet of floor, just leaning against the wall.

Then I heard a roar of a bellow, which sank to a snarl. The snarl roared,

"Isabel! Get the hell up here!"

I kind of dawdled on the stairs, but it was no use. Nothing was safe from Old Eagle Eyes. I should have known she would find it.

It was the incense that did it, I guess. She must have smelled it when I left the closet door open to go downstairs.

Well, they were fit to be tied, although I really must be fair and say that Gog looked magnificent.

Oh, you really should have seen him with his empty eye

sockets flaming, making his jewels sparkle and dance in the shadows, his ruby lips grinning around his big gray teeth, his whole head framed by his gold ball ears with their little red geranium antennas behind them!

Marian shrieked again and again and He turned to her and said,

"Marian, stop that immediately. It is nothing but a stupid prank your sister has put up to frighten you. Did you hear me? Stop that immediately!"

I can never remember if livid means you are red or white, which is handy because He was going both by turns.

Marian finally shut up and I stood staring down at my feet, wondering what would happen next. I was really scared. You never know just what He'll do when he's angry.

I didn't have to wait long. He suddenly grabbed me by the throat. Then He thought the better of that and a second later seized my shoulders. He shook me until I honestly thought my head would come off and at one point He actually lifted me off my feet.

Then he sort of tossed me against the wall where fortunately I bounced off harmlessly.

Marian started to scream again.

He turned to her and looking like He would like to hit her, too.

When she stopped her yodeling He turned back to me.

"Just what in the name of God have you been up to?"

I ducked behind Marian and said I wouldn't say anything unless He promised not to hit me.

The muscles of his jaws were clenching and unclenching but He swallowed hard and said,

"Speak!"

I explained it was my idol. Then, of course, He wanted to know why I built it, so I said it was just for the fun of it.

He asked what was so goddamn funny about an idol and I said I didn't see what harm it could do, especially since He said there wasn't any God.

He picked up Lady Clementine by her slender body and held her at arm's length and asked what in the name of Christ was this supposed to be.

I said it was just a little old bush. I didn't dare tell him the truth about it being a stolen sacrifice. He would have killed me right on my own altar.

He leaned against the wall with his hands in his pockets and bit his lips. He told Marian everything was all right and she must be calm and go downstairs.

After she had gone he turned to me again.

"Get that *abomination* out of my house!"

He kicked Gog to pieces then jumped up and down on the flames of the candles. It was a real desecration, I can tell you.

He went to the window in the box room and opened it and turned to me.

"Did you hear me? Get that *accursed thing* out of my house! Out the window! Then you get down to the yard *on the double* and put the whole lot of it in the garbage cans. Do you understand?"

I said yes. He said get busy and if you ever do anything so monstrous as this again I'll break every bone in your body.

And so I threw my splendid idol out the window and then I went down and put the sad remains in the garbage cans.

I have a confession to make. I have to admit later that for all His shouting and swearing and stamping I felt strangely relieved.

Since I had thought I had seen the fire in the air and on the walls during my trial run, I had been just a little afraid of Gog.

Well, Gog is gone now for sure. My father is a very thorough man.

How are things? I finally gave in, that's how they are, because I just had to talk to Bonnie. Oddly enough when I phoned she said, "Hi, long time no see," as if things were like they used to be.

When I asked her how she was she said her heartburn wasn't so bad but those damned piles were driving her crazy. Then *she* suggested that we would meet under the tree.

It used to be that when I was upset I could curl up in the front seat and put my head on her lap but now we're both too big, so I just leaned my head against her shoulder.

"I know you," she said. "Something's the matter."

I told her all my troubles, especially about my idol, and how He tore it down.

She said, "You built a what?"

I repeated that I had built Gog.

"Honestly, Isabel, I can hardly believe my ears. You must be kidding."

I said I wasn't and explained about finding out if there were a God.

She was so shocked she pushed me away from her and said she had never in her whole life heard of such a terrible thing.

"How could you do anything so horrible?"

It wasn't so difficult. I tried to be rational and explained that I really couldn't think of any other way of finding out for sure if there was a God and if he had struck the Israelites dead for worshiping a golden calf. I said I couldn't think of any alternative.

"No alternative!" she shouted. "What if your mother had found it, you awful girl! Did you ever stop to think what it would have done to her if she'd gone into the box-room closet instead of Marian?"

As a matter of fact, that had never occurred to me. As a further matter of fact I really hadn't counted on old Snoopy finding it either.

"Really, Isabel, that's the most awful thing I have ever heard in my life! Aren't you even sorry?"

"No," I said. I was, but I wasn't going to go around licking *everybody's* boots.

Bonnie surprised me by her attitude, because, like my father, she never goes to church and as far as I know doesn't believe in God, either. If she does, she never mentioned it.

I tried to explain that it was really a scientific experiment, and for her to try and think of me like another Louis Pasteur or Alexander Graham Bell. If God had given me a sign I would have lived my life differently. I'd have cured my mother while I was here and probably gone to heaven when I died. Now I'd never know.

"Never know!" she screeched. "Oh, Isabel! How could you be so terrible! First that crazy old Colonel and that dotty Mrs. Lamb and now the Israelites! Isabel! Can't you find any normal, nice young girls your own age?"

"No," I said. I felt fed up. Everybody yells at me but nobody ever stops to think of my side of the story. I didn't want to do wrong. I wanted to do right. So what happens? Everybody yells and shrieks and carries on about how awful I am. Nobody seems to consider the risk I took; that I might have been struck dead if there was a God and He got mad.

I stayed on my side of the car with my head leaning against the window and looked out at the waves on the beach and didn't speak.

I knew it wouldn't last long. The trouble is I can't stay mad and neither can Bonnie and we both know it.

Finally she pulled me to her and said, only this time in a nice soft voice,

"Oh, you awful rotten kid. Honestly, I don't know what to do with you. It's like some crazy thing Bud would do. I never heard of anybody in the whole world building their own idol. But I suppose if Bud had lived long enough and thought about God instead of all that B.S. about humanity, he would have got around to building his own God if he thought there wasn't one."

She's got it all backwards of course, but there was no point in going over it again so I said, "You're not mad anymore?"

She hugged me, said she guessed not and that I was the limit, then she started to laugh.

"What's so funny?"

"Oh, Isabel! How I wish I could have seen your father's face!'

It was just like old times.

Almost.

I waited about a week before going over to the Colonel's. I would have gone before but I felt rotten about needlessly killing Lady Clementine. And the more I thought about it, the worse it seemed, from the Colonel's viewpoint, I mean. I sure didn't want him ever finding out it was me.

I thought it best to keep up as normal a front as possible, so I went as soon as I got my courage up.

The Colonel met me at the gate.

"He came back," he whispered in my ear, trembling all over. I was pained to see how old and tired he seemed.

"He came back," he repeated. "This time I have proof." He looked over his shoulder and leaned down and whispered, "This time he left footprints."

Without turning his head he jerked his thumb and his head toward the pillaged little greenhouse.

When we got to the billiard room he winked warningly and breathed, "He has invaded Switzerland."

"The billiard room?" I asked in horror. I was appalled. I hadn't even been near it that night.

"I told you he would come back."

It had never occurred to me that he would blame it on Carruthers.

His little red-veined and blue eyes glittered, then he suddenly shouted in a surprisingly loud, deep voice, as if he wanted Carruthers to hear,

"Revenge! That's what he's after!"

He dropped his voice again. "He stole Lady Clementine! He knows how to counterattack." Then he began to whisper again, "But I'm up to him; we'll spike his guns, eh, McMurry?"

He lit the fireplace. It's always chilly in the billiard room but it seemed chillier than ever today, as if Carruthers had actually invaded Switzerland. The Colonel poured us each a drink. Mine was scotch like his but I didn't say anything, although I hate even the smell of whiskey.

"Colonel," I said, "who *is* Carruthers?"

I had asked him many times before but he'd always put me off by mumbling something about the North African campaign.

The Colonel sat holding his head in his shaking hands. Finally he looked up and said very quietly,

"Carruthers was my aide."

"Why has he come back? What does he want? You say revenge, but I don't understand, sir."

"Damn his eyes and his soul, he's come to haunt me."

I thought this over for a long time.

"Carruthers is dead?"

"Yes! He was killed at Wadi Abbas. You remember I told you about the battle there?"

"Yes," I said. "You think it's his ghost that stole Lady Clementine?"

Even his moustache was quivering now.

"Yes. I know it."

I felt sorry for him, and even sorrier that, I guess you could say, I had stolen, murdered; I had murdered Lady Clementine, but I sure as hell wasn't going to tell him the truth.

To make him feel better I said, "Maybe it wasn't his ghost. Maybe he wasn't really killed. Lots of soldiers were missing and turned up later. I saw a movie called *Random Harvest* and everybody thought Ronald Colman was dead, but he wasn't. He just had amnesia and he turned up safe and sound later and married Greer Garson, although he was already married to her but couldn't remember. It was quite complicated. I bet that's what happened to Carruthers."

He gave a horrible laugh.

"He's dead, all right." His voice was grim and steady. For some reason the hair on the back of my neck prickled.

"How can you be so sure?" I asked.

The next thing was the most shocking I ever heard.

He walked over to the inlaid walnut desk below the window, opened a drawer and pulled out a gun. He threw it on the billiard table.

"How am I sure? Because I killed him. I blew Carruthers' brains out with that very gun; that's how I know he is dead."

I thought I was going to faint.

"Do you know why I used a German Luger? If an autopsy was done an enemy bullet would be found."

The room began to spin. I have never been so frightened.

I was the one whispering now.

"Why did you kill Carruthers?"

He got a crafty look on his face and grinned.

"Oh, I saw through him from the beginning. He was an *abomination*!

"That terrible word again. He thought I didn't know. Oh, butter wouldn't melt in Carruthers' beautiful mouth!"

Then he shouted, "Well, there was nothing left of that beautiful face, I can tell you, not after three little messengers from the soldier's God!"

He pointed to the Luger.

"He was a filthy pervert!" he shouted.

I was shaking as much as he was. I had to think of something to help make me move.

I closed my eyes and I thought of the May Spoon and it shone before me like a picture.

I had to get out of there, and I had to be smart.

"I have to go now," I said, and believe it or not, my voice sounded so calm it could have been someone else's.

He didn't even hear me.

"I trusted him, you see. I loved him. Yes, I can say it. I loved him! Alive, he was beautiful and beguiling. But in the end he was just another corpse swelling and popping in the Egyptian sun!"

There were bubbles of spit at the corners of his mouth.

"Good-bye," I said. "I'll see you tomorrow."

Of course I knew I'd never enter that billiard room again. Maybe I wouldn't leave it either. Maybe he'd bury me in the garden—in the hole left by the Black Rose. Poetic justice and just my sort of luck.

He didn't seem to realize I was there anymore and I wasn't going to wait until he did.

I ran up the stairs, through the house, through the garden. My hands shook so much I didn't think I'd be able to unlock the gates, but somehow I did, all the time expecting a bullet in the back of my head.

Would I feel it? How would I know I was dead? Crazy thoughts flashed through my brain.

I ran home.

No one was home except my mother. By the time I got to my room I thought my heart would burst. I lay on my bed and shook and shook.

I couldn't tell anybody about it.

Ever.

It's been five days since I wrote those words. Four of those days were hell.

I was afraid to turn my light out in my bedroom at night in case the Colonel crept in.

When I did fall asleep I had terrible dreams about Carruthers. It was as if the Colonel's haunting was some sort of contagious disease and I had caught it.

Every night I'd wake up from this nightmare sleep, sweating and shaking. I didn't know how it would ever stop or if it would ever end, and I didn't know what to do.

The dreams! I'd see Carruthers as he was in his picture. Tall, brown, and handsome, with that strange faraway look, gazing out over the desert. Then his head would rotate, and I'd be looking at the back of it.

Slowly he'd turn and look at me again, and his face wasn't there.

Then I'd hear the snap of a gun being cocked and the soft footsteps tiptoeing to my door.

Finally, when the door began to swing open slowly, I'd force myself, by willpower alone, to wake up.

I was so desperate I even thought of running away to Aunt Ada.

My father's eyes kept following me around the house. Whenever we were in the same room I'd turn and find Him staring at me.

Finally I shouted, "Leave me alone!"

He came over, looking sort of embarrassed. He said, "If it's about that idol business, well, maybe I reacted a little harshly. I don't mind telling you it scared hell out of me. You see, I was educated by Jesuits. And believe me, they put the fear of God in you forever."

And then He said it.

"I'm sorry."

If ever I needed a father, I needed one now. For the first time in my life I kind of liked Him. I wanted to throw my arms around his waist and hug Him, but we are not a hugging family and I was afraid to. If He pushed me away I don't think I could have stood it.

So I said, "I'm sorry I made Gog."

He shuddered. "For God's sake, child, don't give it a *name*."

Then He chucked me under the chin and said, "Keep punchin', Skookum."

Skookum is a local Indian word which means big or brave.

The next day my ordeal ended at the breakfast table. He was reading the morning paper, holding it up with one hand and his fork with the other. Suddenly He dropped both and said, "Well, I'll be damned."

194

Marian said, "What's the matter?"

"How shocking!" He said.

"What?" cried Marian. "What?"

"It's Isabel's Colonel," He said. "Oh, my God."

"What? What?" Marian again.

He looked at me in a funny, sad way.

"I'm afraid the Colonel is dead, Isabel."

I could feel my face go white.

"Give me the paper."

"Maybe I had better read it to you, it might be easier that way."

"What is it?" shrieked Marian.

"Stop shouting, Marian! Isabel, the Colonel shot himself, and he killed his dog as well."

I let my breath out very slowly and I could feel the blood start to run in my veins again.

"Believe me, I'm very sorry," He said. "Poor old bugger. I wonder why? Well, he *was* a bit odd."

He could say that again. I had to clench my fists and keep them on my lap so they wouldn't see my hands shaking.

"Go on," said Marian. "What else does it say?"

He was reading, when suddenly He looked up at us and said, "Well, I'll be damned!"

"Oh, *Daddy!*" shouted Marian.

"Listen to this! It says, 'Although known locally as Colonel George Paget, he was, in fact, Brigadier General the Honourable George Peregrine Augustus de Vere Paget, third son of the late seventh Earl of Dorminster and brother of the present eighth earl. He served with distinction in the North African campaign during the Second World War, receiving the D.S.C., M.C., K.G.M.B. and O.B.E. No note was left and foul play is not suspected.' "

Marian sat staring at me.

"Wow," she said. "You knew all along, didn't you?"

He said, "Poor fellow. Well, one never knows what goes on in the mind of another human being. I wish I had had the privilege of meeting him."

I have never known Him to speak so highly of anyone in His life, and I have never been so relieved in my life. I know now how it must feel to mount the scaffold, have the black hood placed over your head, the rope around your neck, and then be told you are reprieved.

He said, "Try not to think about it, Isabel. Who knows, perhaps it was for the best. Marian, Isabel has had quite a shock. Why don't you do the big thing and do her chores for her today?"

He handed me a bill. "Here, take this. Go to a movie or something. It will take your mind off the whole awful thing."

The nightmare was over and I felt rotten. Not for the Colonel; I felt rotten about Rommel. He was really an awfully nice dog when you got to know him.

I sat on my bed for a long time and looked up at the real Anne. "Do you think it was my fault?" I asked her. "Shouldn't I feel just a bit guilty?"

Her big sad eyes looked down at me from her lovely face.

"I just feel guilty about not feeling guilty, if you know what I mean."

I sighed. "Well, I think I know now how you felt when the Gestapo were coming up the stairs. I wish you had been as lucky as me."

The Fates harrow me. I am not exaggerating. It just doesn't seem possible they could hound one person so much.

196

Last week I was in the village looking in the window of an antique shop. In front, on a table, was a silver tea service.

I heard a man's voice behind me say,

"No darling, it is not Victorian. It is Georgian."

Then a woman's voice said, "I'm sure they did *not* have the melon pattern in the Georges' time."

"Want to bet?" said the man's voice.

I turned.

There he was.

And standing next to the last of the Romanovs, the sun glinting on her long platinum hair and casting magic tinges on her shining, biscuit-coloured skin, was Jane Lonsdale.

They were holding hands. He leaned and nuzzled his face against her hair, then kissed her.

She stood back. Looking into his eyes, she raised their laced fingers and slowly kissed and sucked each one of his, their eyes as locked as their fingers.

Then she saw me, smiled, and dropped his hand.

"Why, hello, Isabel. How are you?"

How was I? She had just destroyed my world, that's how I was. I couldn't answer. I raised my eyes to him. He looked at me without recognition, giving me that empty smile polite people give to strangers.

Why, of all the people in the whole world, did he pick Jane Lonsdale? She was what I wanted to look like, wanted to be like, wanted to act like, wanted to think like.

And there she was now, my double, standing in my place, at his side, where I wanted to be. It wasn't fair to hate her because she had never done me any harm, but hate her I did, suddenly and terribly.

"Is anything the matter?" she asked when I didn't answer her.

Anything the matter? No, nothing at all. They were like

Adam and Eve in Paradise, perfect for each other in every way.

What was skinny, dumb, clumsy old me, with my clothes that are either too big or too small doing here, even looking at them? I didn't belong in their Eden. The gods would blind me for daring to intrude.

"Are you okay?" she said.

I looked at him and then away. Surely it was like looking at the sun and my eyes would melt in my head like ice.

"I thought you were going to Europe or Africa or some-place," I said.

"Oh," she laughed, "not for a while. I'd like you to meet my fiancé, Jack. Jack, this is my friend Isabel."

Betrothed again and Fraser Schinbein is not yet festering in his shroud!

I wanted to say I am not your friend, Jane Lonsdale. But I didn't. I am always polite, on the surface, at least. Underneath I am often very rude. I turned and walked away.

"Hey!" she called after me, "hey, Isabel, what's the matter? Come back."

I just kept walking.

I cried all night. I thought my heart would break. Jane Lonsdale, the day before I turned around and saw you there I thought you were the most perfect woman in the world. You didn't love Fraser Schinbein and I don't think you love him. For you people are just things to while away the time with.

I didn't know what jealousy was before. It simply tears you apart. It rises in your throat like vomit so you wish you could spew it out but it just stays there, burning and hurting. And there's nothing you can do about it except cut the source of it—your heart—out.

I suppose I could write to Ann Landers about this but I

know she would only reply with something infuriatingly sensible, and there's no sensible cure for jealousy.

Things very quiet for this last week. Getting ready for the next round, I guess. Yesterday I learned that the ancient Russians used to dye their eyeballs blue. I think I'll phone Bonnie. It looks like hell will freeze over before she will call me.

When I came into the kitchen after school yesterday everything was very quiet. From somewhere in the house I heard a muffled sound of weeping.

I called but nobody answered me. In the living room Marian was sitting with a handkerchief stuffed against her mouth and she was crying. Then Dr. Wilkes, our family doctor, came into the room.

I looked around and I felt trapped and frightened. "Where's my mother?" I asked Dr. Wilkes.

"Now, take it easy," he said. "She's all right."

Marian took the handkerchief away from her mouth and said, "It's your fault!"

I walked into the den. He was sitting there with His head in His hands.

"Where's my mother?"

He didn't even raise His head. Dr. Wilkes followed me in. "Your mother has gone to a hospital," he told me.

I ran over to my father and tried to drag His hands away from His face.

"What did you do to her?" I screamed. "You killed her! You killed her like you killed Peggy!"

He took his hands away from his face and stood up. Then He pushed me away with one hand. He sort of sighed and said to Dr. Wilkes, "Take her away."

Marian came in and stood in the doorway and yelled, "It's all your fault! If you hadn't told her she'd be all right!" Dr. Wilkes turned to her and told her to be quiet.

I just stood there and screamed so Dr. Wilkes grabbed me by the arm and dragged me upstairs to my room.

Then he got out a hypodermic needle and swabbed my arm. I felt the prick of the needle going in.

"You'll feel better in a minute. Listen to what I say. Your mother has been taken to a hospital, just as I told you downstairs."

He stood looking down at me.

"Your shock therapy worked," he said. "For the first time since Bud's death, she is responding. I have confidence that she will make a recovery now, with psychiatric aid, whereas before the situation was hopeless. She could not be reached. And as long as no contact could be made with her, she could not be helped.

"Don't feel guilty about what you did. You are the only one around here who used your head and in the end it will all have been for the best. I'm going to leave you now. You'll be asleep in a few minutes."

He patted my head then walked to the door where he stopped. "Don't be too hard on your Father or Marian. They are upset too, you know."

After he left I lay looking at the real Anne. She seemed alive and I was dead. The drug I guess. I fell asleep.

I didn't think this house could be so empty without my mother. She never said much but she was always happy and busy. And she was always *here*.

It's like a big, dirty tomb now. I didn't realize how much work she did. There seems to be no end to the amount of washing and ironing and dusting and waxing and vacuuming and windows to be done. What with that and the cooking, Marian and I are doing a lousy job and He is raising hell.

He does absolutely *nothing*. Things aren't helped by the fact that the only thing I can make is fudge and the only thing Marian can make is crepes suzette. Every meal is a bigger disaster than the last one.

Yesterday He decided to take things in his own hands and cook dinner. After dirtying every pot and pan in the kitchen He came up with some awful mess of sour cream and mushrooms and sliced beef and onions, only the sour cream had gone bad and in a rage He threw the whole thing out the back door, got in the car, and drove off. We were left with the mess to clean up and no dinner. We fried up some eggs that were in the fridge and I made a salad. Marian found a can of chocolate pudding in the cupboard and we dined alone.

It was quite cozy.

Marian seems to be improving. Well, as Mr. Cooper-Smythe would say, there is room for improvement.

Dr. Wilkes phoned Marian and said Mother is making remarkable progress already and we will be able to visit her soon. *He* visits her three times a week. He never tells us how she is and neither of us dares to ask Him.

Honestly! Has fate any cream pies left to throw at me? Well, here it is. He has accepted a teaching post in an English university and has decided that Marian and I are to go to Grange House, a very exclusive boarding school here. We have already been given a long lecture on the costs and sacrifices He will have to make in His old age for the fees, board, and uniforms.

The idea of going to that school frightens me so much I feel sick. I won't know anyone except Marian. Marian is, of course, looking forward to it because there's a scholarship to the Sorbonne and naturally she will win it.

Oh, if only things would stop changing, for just a little while.

I have been moping around so much Marian says I give her the willies.

I said, "Yeah? It's okay for you. You've only got a year before you graduate, but I'll be there for the rest of my natural life. He's dumping us, like we were a couple of mangy pups He was dropping off at the pound. And what about Mumma? Why does He hate us, Marian?"

"Oh, Isabel. Don't you understand anything? Mumma will be well soon. Sure He's mean, but He doesn't hate us. We bore Him. It's as simple as that. But He'll get bored with England, too, and besides, when He's had a year to add up those school bills he'll be back like a bird dog."

I phoned Bonnie and when I asked how she was she said, "Awful. As if these damned piles aren't enough, my damned varicose veins are whooping it up again. Believe you me, this baby is sure going to be an only child."

I told her about my mother and she said that was fine, or maybe she said it was too bad. I don't remember. Whichever it was it was as if they both sounded the same to her.

I told her about the school and started to cry.

She said, "Oh, come on, now, Isabel. Stop being such a baby. Lots of kids would give their eye teeth to go to a school like that, with those beautiful uniforms."

She doesn't care and the uniforms are horrible. Navy tams and blazers and pleated tartan skirts and knee socks. I'll bet if they cropped my head like an old-fashioned convict and the canvas uniforms had big black and white horizontal stripes, she'd still think they were beautiful.

I said, "But I don't know anybody there except Marian and she doesn't count because she is so far ahead of me in school. I didn't think things could be worse, but they are."

Bonnie said, "Oh, for God's sake, Isabel, will you ever stop dramatizing *everything*! You'll be fine at that school."

Then she said good-bye and good luck. Just like that. Just like I was anybody. She doesn't care. Nobody does.

Diaries are stupid and I'm tired of keeping this one. I told Marian so and she looked kind of worried. As a matter of fact, for the last two or three days, she has been worried about me because I've stayed mad and sad for four days, and I could never manage to do either for that long before.

"I think you should keep your diary. It's healthy and will help you get rid of your awful angst."

"What's angst?"

We were in the kitchen and Marian was making a peanut-butter sandwich. She blushed furiously and then began to laugh. "I dunno," she said. "I heard it from Rhea."

If I hadn't made up my mind not to, I would have laughed too. It's the first time I ever heard Marian admit she didn't know something she said.

"You make the tea," she said. "After all, things could be worse."

"How?"

"What do you mean, 'how'! You're alive, aren't you?"

I didn't see what that had to do with it and said so.

203

"What's the very worst thing that could happen to you?"

"Going to Grange House."

Marian stamped her foot. "Oh, really, you are the most irritating child I have ever met! Think! Think! Think!"

Then as He says, the penny dropped.

"You mean—you mean—I could die?"

"Yup," she said in what, considering the subject, sounded like a very cheerful manner to me.

I sat thinking, thinking, thinking. Then I started phantasizing.

After a while Marian asked me what I was thinking about.

"About being dead, of course. Well, not being dead, but dying. How awfully sad it would be for all of you."

"Har, har," she said.

"No, I mean it. I'm sort of writing a story in my head.

"Listen." Then I told her my story.

I lie in my hospital bed surrounded by banks of flowers sent by my many friends. My illness is very rare and has baffled famous doctors the world over and I've even been on TV. Fortunately it is painless and has made me very pretty, which is nice because most people get ugly as they die.

My parents never leave me. They hover by my bedside ceaselessly weeping and holding hands over my wasted body.

Marian has begged forgiveness for her many meannesses and I have forgiven her.

"Whaddya mean! Meanness?" she shouted.

"Oh, all right. I take that back."

The Camorras have all been to see me and brought bouquets of flowers and begged me to reinstate myself and be their president. I have said I would think about it.

Beatrice has asked forgiveness too but I feel that would be going too far, even for someone like me who never holds grudges. But I sort of let her off the hook with a lecture about her rottenness and said I hoped she would improve before facing her Maker, whom I shall be seeing soon.

Conn O'Rourke came and stood at the foot of my bed. His grief insupportable and he is led away weeping.

Bonnie couldn't come because she just had her baby, which is a boy and won't get to be called Ann, which serves her right.

Mr. Romanov comes bearing a huge heart of red roses. He has spent a fortune tracing me with an army of private detectives. He had almost given up hope when it occurred to him to trace me through my adopted name of McMurry.

"Your what?" interrupted Marian.

"Oh, shut up," I said. "This is the best part."

Mr. Romanov tells me he has a twin brother who goes around West Vancouver impersonating him. I comfort him and tell him we will meet in heaven, which makes him cry all the more. He is just like Heathcliff only not dark and mean. He takes off his gold and diamond ring and places it on my withered finger. I tell him I will be buried in it.

He cries that he cannot bear it and will join me in the grave.

Marian doubled up with laughter. "That's against the law. Tell him to try the city garbage disposal."

"Will you quit interrupting?"

I make him promise not to do it. I tell him to go on living for my sake as long as he doesn't enjoy himself too much with other women. He gives me his solemn oath that neither dawn nor dusk would ever give him pleasure.

I bequest him the May Spoon and my embroidery. I leave everything else to Marian.

"Gee, thanks a million," she said. "I can hardly wait."

She laughed till tears ran down her face.

"Oh, Jeez. Honestly, Isabel. Can't you do anything in proportion? I ask you a simple thing, to think of being alive instead of dead, and you come up with a whole scenario that makes Hamlet sound like an Andy Hardy rerun. Oh, for Pete's sake, Isabel! I didn't mean anything. Actually, Isabel, I have to admit your death was sort of moving at times. But everything is going to work out."

"It will not!" I shouted. "Everything is going to be lousy as usual, including that school!"

"Do you want a peanut-butter sandwich?" Marian asked. "There's some strawberry jam left to go with it."

"No, thank you." I said with icy politeness.

She turned around, a spoonful of peanut butter in her hand beginning to drop.

"Listen," she said. "I've got an idea. A really good one. But you've got to promise to cooperate and for God's sake, will you pleeeeeeeease quit whining?"

"You're dropping peanut butter all over the floor and so what's your wonderful idea?"

She got a paper napkin off the top of the fridge and as she was kneeling down wiping up the floor, she looked up at me, and there was no laughter in her eyes.

"We'll stick it out for six months at that school and if you still really hate it, we'll leave."

"Where would we leave to?" I asked.

"To England, of course."

"You're kidding," I said.

"No, I am not. Just leave the details to me."

Marian *never* tells lies.

"But—how—would we––," I said.

"Leave it up to me. Now, are you finally cheered up?"

She finished cleaning the floor and as she was washing her hands at the sink she turned to me again.

"We'll go to Buckingham Palace. Well, not in it, of course. And we'll go to see the Chamber of Horrors at Madam Tussaud's. You'll love that! And Hyde Park and the jewels in the Tower of London. All the things we've seen on TV."

She offered me half her sandwich and I began to chew it automatically.

"We might even get up north to where your precious Brontës lived."

"Haworth Parsonage? Really?"

"Sure. Why not? England isn't like Canada. It doesn't take you three or four days to cross the country by train. You can get anywhere there in few hours."

"Wow!" I said.

So things aren't as bad as I thought they were. As Marian says, you can stand just about anything for six months, except maybe a toothache.

But I really meant it about closing this diary. I can't think of anything else to say except that maybe I should quit exaggerating so much.

To think that only yesterday I was utterly despairing and now *I am going to England!*

Miss Swanson would probably say my ending is contrived.

Next to Mumma and Mr. Romanov and maybe Marian, I still love Miss Swanson more than anybody, but you have to admit she was never very good at endings.

So, hopefully I'll say good-bye for now.

(Did you get that? Hopeably you'll understand and I'll be famous. For something.)

Yours sincerely,
A. Carleon